"No one but Elizabeth Laird could have written this book. She has lived in the Middle East. She knows it, feels it, loves it, grieves for it, and hopes for it. Read *A Little Piece of Ground*, and we know what it is to feel oppressed, to feel fear every day. And we should know, for this is how much of the world lives.

We are apt to see events in Palestine and Israel as television drama; violent and repetitive. We are distant from it. But in this book we are taken into Ramallah: we live there, no longer mere observers, but involved as we should be.

A fine book, and a daring book."

—Michael Morpurgo, Britain's Children's Laureate

"This story of how it feels to be under the heel of an occupier and how it affects day-to-day life is an oddly homely one. We get to care about this boy and his family and, yes, to loathe their oppressors—and I say that as one who lived in Israel for years and has written the story of terrorism in that area for children from the Jewish side.... I know it is a good book and needs to be read by others like me."

—Lynne Reid Banks, author of *The Indian in the Cupboard*

Also by Elizabeth Laird

A Little Piece of Ground

Elizabeth Laird
with Sonia Nimr

**Illustrations by
Bill Neal**

Haymarket Books
Chicago, IL

Haymarket Books wishes to extend its gratitude to Jane Jewell for her unceasing support for the publishing of this book. In recognition of her efforts, we would like to dedicate this edition of *A Little Piece of Ground* to the memory of Rachel Corrie.

Published in the United States in 2006 by Haymarket Books
P.O. Box 180165, Chicago, IL 60618
www.haymarketbooks.org

LIBRARY OF CONGRESS CATALOGING IN PUBLICATION DATA
Laird, Elizabeth.
A little piece of ground / Elizabeth Laird ; with Sonia Nimr.
Summary: During the Israeli occupation of Ramallah in the West Bank of Palestine, twelve-year-old Karim and his friends create a secret place for themselves where they can momentarily forget the horrors of war.
ISBN-13: 978-1-931859-38-7 (trade paper)
ISBN-10: 1-931859-38-8
1. Arab-Israeli conflict--Juvenile fiction. [1. Arab-Israeli conflict--Fiction.
2. West Bank--Fiction.] I. Nimr, Sonia. II. Title.
PZ7.L1579Li 2006
[Fic]--dc22
2006008707

Printed in Canada

4 6 8 10 9 7 5

A packet of teaching resources for educators is available for download from www.haymarketbooks.org/laird.html.

This book has been published with the generous support of the Wallace Global Fund.

For Kays
and all the children of Palestine

This is a story about Palestinian boys living under the Israeli military occupation. Theirs is a particular experience, in a particular time and place, but all such occupations are harsh, causing great suffering to the occupied people, and misery to the occupying army. The boys in this book stand for all who live their lives in such circumstances and manage, against the odds, to go on growing up.

Chapter One

K arim sat on the edge of his bed, his head framed by the mass of soccer posters that covered the wall. He was frowning at the piece of paper in his hand.

The ten best things that I want to do (or be) in my life, he had written, *by Karim Aboudi, 15 Jaffa Apartments, Ramallah, Palestine.* Carefully, he underlined it.

Underneath, in his best handwriting, he listed:

1. *Champion soccer player of the entire world (even I can dream).*
2. *Extremely cool, popular, and good-looking and at least six feet, two inches tall (or taller than Jamal, anyway).*
3. *The liberator of Palestine and a national hero.*
4. *Famous TV presenter or actor (famous, anyway).*
5. *Best-ever creator of new computer games.*
6. *My own person, allowed to do what I like without parents and big brothers and teachers on my back all the time.*
7. *Inventor of an acid formula to dissolve reinforced steel as used in tanks and helicopter gunships (Israeli ones).*
8. *Stronger than Joni and my other friends (this is not asking much).*

He stopped and began to chew the end of his pen. In the distance, the sound of an ambulance siren wailed through the afternoon air. He lifted his head and stared out of the window. His eyes, large and dark, peered out from under the straight black hair that framed his slim, tanned face.

He started writing again.

> 9. *Alive. Plus, if I have to get shot, only in places that heal up. Not in the head or spine, inshallah.*
> 10.

But number ten defeated him. He decided to keep the slot free in case a good idea came to him later.

He read through what he'd written and sat for a while, tapping the end of the pen against the collar of his striped sweatshirt, then he took a fresh sheet of paper. More quickly this time, he wrote:

> *The ten things I don't want to do (or be)*
> 1. *Not a shopkeeper like Baba.*
> 2. *Not a doctor, like Mama keeps saying I should. (Why? She knows I hate blood.)*
> 3. *Not short.*
> 4. *Not married to a girl like Farah.*
> 5. *Not shot in the back and stuck in a wheelchair for the rest of my life like that boy who used to go to my school.*
> 6. *Not covered in zits like Jamal.*
> 7. *Not having our house flattened by Israeli tanks and ending up in some lousy tent.*
> 8. *Not having to go to school. At all.*
> 9. *Not living under occupation. Not being stopped all the time by Israeli soldiers. Not being scared. Not being trapped indoors.*
> 10. *Not dead.*

He read his lists through again. They weren't quite right.

There were things, important things, that he'd left out, he was sure of it.

He heard raised voices outside the door. His brother, Jamal, was arguing with their mother. He would come into their shared bedroom in a minute and Karim's moment of peace would be over.

He reached down for the box under his bed, in which he kept his private things, ready to stow his lists inside it, but before he could squirrel them away, Jamal had burst into the room.

It was obvious at first glance that Jamal was in a bad mood. His brown eyes, under the wedge of black hair that fell across his forehead, snapped with irritation. Karim tried to hide his lists behind his back, but Jamal lunged forwards and whisked them out of his hands.

"What's all this secrecy about, huh?" he said. "What are you plotting, you little creep?"

Karim jumped up and tried to grab the sheets of paper back again, but Jamal, who was tall for his seventeen years, was holding them above his head, out of Karim's reach. Karim dived at his brother and pulled at the belt loop of his jeans, trying to wrestle him down onto his bed, but Jamal kept him off easily with one hand, and, still holding the lists out of reach, read through them both.

Karim waited, his face burning, for the scornful comments that he knew would come. They did.

"Champion soccer player? You?" sneered Jamal. "With your two left feet? I think I can see you scoring a goal in the World Cup—or not. You? Liberator of Palestine? With your brains—or lack of?"

Karim swallowed. There was no point in fighting with Jamal. The best thing was to pretend he didn't care.

"Don't worry," he said, as casually as he could. "Jealousy is a natural emotion. When I'm world-famous I'll be good to you. I won't hold anything you say against you, not even that crack about my feet, which is totally unfair because I can cream a ball in between the goalposts like Zinedine Zidane any time I like."

Jamal threw the pieces of paper back to him. He was bored with the subject already.

"So you ought to be able to," he said, "seeing as how you've probably spent at least a year of your life kicking that damned soccer ball against the wall downstairs, on and on and on, driving everyone in this building totally nuts."

Cheated out of a good fight with his little brother, he began to box the air, kicking Karim's nearly new best sneakers out of the way and shuffling around in the small space between the beds as if it was a miniature boxing ring.

Karim went to the window and stared down at the ground, five stories below. An empty plot lay next to the apartment block. It had been flattened, ready for the builders to start work, but nothing had happened there so far. Karim had made it his own, his personal soccer field, the place where he played his special game.

He could feel his legs twitching as he pressed his face against the cool glass. With all his being, he longed to be down there, doing what he loved best, kicking the ball against the wall, losing himself in the rhythm of it.

Kick, bounce, catch-ball-on-end-of-foot, kick, bounce....

When the game went well, his mind would click into neutral. His head would empty out, and his legs and arms would take over. The rhythm would satisfy and soothe him.

Jamal had flopped down onto his bed, stretching out his long, slender legs.

"Get away from the window," he growled at Karim. "They'll see you. They might take a pot shot."

Karim turned his head and looked in the other direction. The Israeli tank that had been squatting at the crossroads just below the apartment block for days now had moved a few yards closer. A soldier was sitting on top of it, his gun cradled in his arms. Beside the tank were three other men, one crouching down, talking into a cell phone.

There was no chance, none at all, that he'd be able to go outside and play his game while the tank was there. Since a Palestinian

10

gunman had shot two people in an Israeli café two weeks ago, the Israelis had set up another curfew, which meant that the whole city had been locked down. Everyone in Ramallah had been trapped indoors for those two weeks, unable to go out (except for a two-hour break once or twice a week) by night or day. If anyone tried—if they so much as stuck a foot out of their front door—the soldiers would open fire and blow it away. Jamal was right. Even standing by the window was dangerous.

He turned away. He wished now that he hadn't looked down at his soccer field. It had made him long to be outside, to be able to run and jump, to swing his arms and kick.

"Anyway," he said to Jamal, "I haven't noticed you being so fantastic at scoring yourself."

Jamal turned his head to stare at him.

"What are you talking about?"

"You're a lousy shot. You know you are," Karim said daringly. "I saw you and your friends throwing stones at the tanks last week. You missed, every time. And don't pretend you weren't aiming at them, because you were."

Jamal sat up and swung his legs over the side of the bed, pleased to have an excuse for a wrestling bout at last.

"You little spy. You've been following me again."

He advanced on Karim, his arms outstretched. Karim shifted away, shuffling up to the head of his bed, wrinkling the scarlet blanket with his white-socked feet, his back against the wall, his hands held up in surrender.

"Lay off me, will you? I won't tell Mama. Not if you leave me alone." He registered with satisfaction the look of caution that had crossed Jamal's face. "And," he went on, "I won't tell Baba either, if you give me one hour of totally unrestricted time on the computer without a single interruption. No, two."

Disgusted, Jamal retreated. Karim could see that he was searching for something cutting to say, and failing. With one hunch of his shoulder, he turned away to the table, grabbed his headphones, hurled himself down onto his bed and clamped them to his ears.

Thrilled with his triumph, Karim jumped up and settled himself at the computer, which took up almost the whole of the table between the two beds. He would do it this time. He would get up to Level 5 in Lineman. He'd nearly managed it last week, but then there'd been a power cut and the computer had crashed just as victory was in sight.

He pushed the tottering pile of textbooks to the edge of the table. He had lists of English words to learn, as well as the dates of the Arab Conquests.

"They can stop you coming to school," his teacher had said, before the curfew had been imposed, "but don't let them stop you learning. Work at home. Your future is Palestine's. Your country needs you. Don't forget it."

He'd tried to work once or twice, but it had been impossible to concentrate for long, with Jamal coming in and out of the room all the time, and Farah and Sireen, his two little sisters, noisily playing in the living room next door. After a few minutes, he'd usually ended up leafing through old comics and weaving delightful daydreams, imagining, for example, that Jamal was a million miles away, preferably in a space capsule endlessly orbiting around the planet Jupiter—or Saturn, he didn't mind which—and that the computer was his and his alone.

And now, for the next two hours, it was.

When my two hours are up I'll do some real work on biology, he told himself, as he stared at the screen, waiting for the game to boot up.

Peace settled on the room. Jamal had got up and gone back into the sitting room, to settle himself on the old red velvet sofa and watch the news with his father. Sireen, who was four and had been crying all morning, had stopped at last, and Farah, who was eight, seemed to have gone across the landing to play with her best friend, Rasha, who lived in the apartment opposite.

The game began. At once, he was totally absorbed.

The opening moves were familiar. He'd played Lineman often enough to go through them almost automatically. Soon, though, he was doing the harder stuff. He tensed over the keyboard, his eyes boring into the screen, his fingers responding with lightning speed to his brain's commands. Slowly he was climbing through the levels. This time, he might really make it.

The door of the bedroom opened. He didn't look around, but he sensed his mother's presence. He needn't need to turn and look at her to know that a deep frown was scoring her forehead between her sharp black brows.

"You want an education, Karim, or you want to grow up like your uncle Bashir?" She paused, waiting for an answer. Karim said nothing. "You want to mend roads for the next fifty years? Break your back in the hot sun, shoveling dirt?" Another silence. "Suit yourself. Don't expect me to wash your dirty clothes for the rest of your life, that's all."

He grunted, having barely heard what she had said. She sighed with exasperation and closed the door again. The game went on. One by one, the targets fell, and level succeeded level. Breathless, almost dizzy, Karim willed the screen to obey him, and when at last it exploded into stars as he reached the highest level, his head seemed to explode too.

"Ye-e-ess!" he yelled, and he slammed out of the bedroom into the sitting room and danced around the rest of his family, punching the air in triumph. "I did it! I did it! Level Five! First time ever! Champion of the world! Victory is mine! Yield and obey, all lesser mortals!"

Jamal got up off the sofa.

"Level Five? In Lineman? Let me see."

He pushed past Karim into the bedroom.

Hassan Aboudi, Karim's father, was sitting bent over on the sofa, staring at the TV screen, watching people wailing at a funeral. The announcer's solemn voice seemed to fill the room.

Five Palestinians, including two children, died during clashes between Israeli soldiers and stone-throwing youths in the West Bank town of Nablus this morning.

Hassan Aboudi turned to look angrily at Karim.

"Stop that noise right now," he snapped. "Get back to your homework or I'll take the damned computer away."

Lamia, Karim's mother, was half reclining on an easy chair nearby. Her legs were crossed and a pink slipper dangled from her raised foot. Sireen had been sleeping against her chest, but she woke at the noise and struggled in her mother's arms, beginning to cry fretfully again. The mark of a button from Lamia's red blouse showed clearly on the little girl's cheek.

"Now look what you've done," Lamia said reproachfully, lifting the damp black curls off Sireen's hot little forehead. "You know how sick she is. Don't you remember what an earache feels like? I had just gotten her settled, poor little thing. You might think what it's like for other people sometimes, Karim. Or is that really too much to ask?"

Jamal lounged back into the room, his hands in his pockets.

"It was only Level Four, you sad person. Thought you were one of the big boys, huh? Well, I've got news for you. You aren't."

Karim felt his pleasure and triumph drain away and the miserable sense of imprisonment that the game had kept at bay for the last two happy hours closed in on him again.

"I hate you! You're lying! You know you are!" he shouted, aiming a blow at Jamal's chest.

Jamal laughed and ducked out of the way. Karim rushed back to look at the computer screen, but Jamal had turned the machine off. Now he couldn't prove a thing.

Desperate to be alone, to get away from his whole unbearable family, he went to the front door, opened it, stepped outside, and closed it after him. The landing and stairs weren't much, but at least he'd be on his own for a bit.

Almost at once the door behind him opened again.

"Karim," his father said, his voice tense with anxiety, "what do you think you're doing? Get back in here right now."

"I'm not going outside, Baba," Karim said. "I'll stay on the landing. I just—I need to be on my own for a minute."

His father's face softened.

"All right, but only for a little while. Don't go near the window. Don't let them see you. Keep yourself out of sight. Come back in after ten minutes or your mother will start going crazy on me."

The sound of the TV news followed Karim out through the open door of the apartment.

Israeli troops shelled a refugee camp in Gaza this morning, killing nine Palestinians, including a three-year-old child. Five Israeli women died and three children were badly injured when a Palestinian gunman opened fire in a crowded shopping street in Jerusalem this morning. A spokesman....

He pulled the door closed behind him, shutting the voice out, then balled his fist and punched at the wall, painfully grazing his knuckles.

Chapter Two

Three more eternal days passed before the curfew was lifted and then the break was only for two hours. A soldier on the tank down below shouted the news through a megaphone.

"From six o'clock in the evening for two hours," his voice boomed, "going out of your houses is permitted."

Lamia let out a sob of relief.

"If they'd kept us penned up in here one more day," she said, wringing out a cool cloth to lay on Sireen's head, "this child's ear infection would have gone into her brain. Her temperature's been way up for three days now. And anyway, we've almost run out of food."

Her husband was already on the telephone. He replaced the receiver and turned to her.

"Dr. Selim's given me the name of the right antibiotic. I'll take her down to the pharmacy as soon as we can get out. He says to start her with a double dose tonight."

He went off to his bedroom, shaking his head.

"Punishing children," Karim heard him mutter. "Let God punish them."

It wasn't only Sireen's ear that was likely to be saved by the break in the curfew, thought Karim. Just one more day of imprisonment and there would have been a massacre of the entire Aboudi family. He himself would have personally murdered both Farah and Jamal, his parents would have murdered each other, and the whole family would have ganged up to murder him.

He fished his cell phone out from the mess of stuff on the shelf above his bed and punched in the number of Joni, his best friend.

"I've got to take my homework into school and get a whole lot more," he told him. "Have you?"

"No. My teacher called. He's coming by my father's shop. He says he'll pick it up there."

"You are lucky," Karim said enviously. "I wish I went to your school. They're much stricter at mine. There's only two hours. We won't have time to meet."

"Yes, we will. I'll come down to your school. I'll meet you at the gate."

The last few minutes before six o'clock came seemed to Karim like the longest since the curfew had begun. He felt like a can of Pepsi that had been shaken up and was full of fizz, just bursting to shoot out in a wild, frothing spray.

By 5:55 the whole family was poised to rush out. Lamia waited, impatiently smoothing down the blue material of her skirt, her purse in her hand. Hassan was holding Sireen, ready to run with her down to the pharmacy. Farah was frantically searching her bedroom for the pink top she was determined to put on before she skipped out to play in the apartment courtyard with the other children of the building. Karim, in clean jeans and a fresh sweatshirt, was reluctantly putting together his homework. It was only now that he came to look at the scrappy bits of paper and the half-finished exercises in his books that he realized how little he'd managed to do.

The hands on the fancy pendulum clock that hung on the living room wall moved around to six at last, and with it came the longed-for revving of the tanks' engines. With the front door ajar, everyone listened eagerly as the huge machines clanked away from the street corner and retreated to the bottom of the hill.

Jamal, his thick hair freshly gelled, was the first out. He jumped down the stairs six at a time, with Karim right after him.

"Karim! Meet me at the supermarket at seven thirty!" his mother screeched after him. "I can't carry all the shopping back on my own. And Jamal, if you're not back before eight, I'll... "

But neither boy heard what she planned to do. They were out on the street already.

The fresh air on his face, the wind in his hair and the wonderful liberty to run and jump intoxicated Karim. He had taken the bottom flight of steps in one wild leap and now he was jumping up and down and running around the parking lot in a wide joyful circle.

Jamal had taken off at the speed of a bullet, but instead of going up the hill, towards the school, he was racing down it. Karim stopped running and watched him, eyes narrowed. He guessed what Jamal had in mind. He would be meeting up with Basim and his other friends and making for the wrecked bus park which the soldiers had taken over and where they had their base. He could imagine the great armored machines lying down there, like a row of green scaly monsters, crouched, waiting to crawl back up the hill and pin the people of Ramallah down in their houses again when the two precious hours of freedom were up.

Karim's stomach lurched with fright at the thought of what Jamal and his friends would be doing. They'd be picking up stones and hurling them at the tanks, shouting insults at the soldiers inside. The soldiers would have their fingers on the triggers of their rifles and they'd wait for a bit, and then they'd get angry, or they'd panic, and they'd fire. Someone, sure as anything, would get hurt, or even killed.

If it's Jamal, thought Karim, he'll be a martyr, and I'll be so proud of him I'll never, ever think anything bad about him again.

He had set off by now and was running fast towards the school. With luck, it wouldn't take long to hand in his schoolwork and grab the next assignment.

Joni was at the school gates already. He was moving bizarrely, spinning and kicking on his sturdy legs, and punching out with his plump arms. The boys who were streaming past him on their way in through the battered old gates looked at him oddly, but Karim, used to Joni's habit of practicing karate kicks, was unimpressed.

He had run fast for the last ten minutes and, unused to exercise after the long days indoors, was so winded that for a moment or two he couldn't speak. He bent over, gasping for breath.

When at last he straightened up, he found Joni's foot high up in the air, four inches from his face. Karim pushed it down.

"Listen," he said, "I got to Level Five in Lineman."

"You didn't."

"I did."

He was impressed, Karim could tell, but he was trying not to show it.

Joni followed Karim up the stairs towards the upper row of classrooms. Other boys were crowding round the open doors.

"Where's Mr. Mohammed?" Karim asked one of them.

"Not here," he said. "He hasn't turned up. He's not coming."

"Great!" Karim disliked his stern teacher. He grabbed Joni's arm. "There's no point in hanging around here any longer. We can go and play soccer. I've got to meet my mother at the supermarket, but she won't be ready till at least seven thirty. We've got nearly an hour."

A crowd of boys was already assembled on the soccer field behind the school and a game had just begun. There was no time to organize teams. Everyone joined in, playing around, dodging and passing and shooting at the goal.

For the first few minutes Karim felt clumsy and breathless, running as if his legs were as stiff and weak as matchsticks, missing the goals he tried to score and being easily outmaneuvered by anyone who tried to tackle him. Then, suddenly, he felt his skill coming back. Power vibrated through him. A rare magic tingled through his feet.

The light was going now, the sun sinking fast towards the horizon. The white stone walls of Ramallah were turning a pale yellow. Soon they would be golden, then pink. In more normal times, the smell of frying onions would be wafting from open windows and music would drift across the town from a dozen radios. Tonight, though, the return of darkness would bring only the soldiers and the tanks, the occasional burst of gunfire and the wail of sirens.

Karim had just scored a peach of a goal and was enjoying his triumph with squawks of delight when the caretaker came running round the side of the building. His red and white checked keffiyeh headdress was flapping round his shoulders and he was waving his arms urgently.

"Out! You've all got to get out now!" he shouted. "I'm shutting up the compound! I've got to get home before the tanks come back!"

Karim felt a thump of anger and savagely kicked at the ground. The precious two hours of normal life were over. There was no telling when the next time would be.

Together, he and Joni went out through the school gates and set off towards the supermarket.

"Hey," said Joni suddenly. "Your brother's over there."

Karim looked up, surprised. Jamal was a ways ahead, further along the road, with a gang of friends. Sharply dressed, they were standing around the door of the Internet cafe, their favorite place in town.

He was relieved. There must have been no violent clash down by the tanks today.

"Isn't that your sister, too? Look, isn't that Violette?" he said, pointing towards a girl in tight pink trousers with swinging shoulder-length hair who was coming out of a shop on the far side of the street.

Joni looked up quickly and dropped his eyes again, then he sidled around to walk on Karim's far side.

"What's the matter with you?" Karim said, surprised.

"I don't want her to see me," mumbled Joni. "You don't know Violette."

"Sure I do. I've known her all my life."

"You don't. She's just totally embarrassing. Last time I met her in the street she was with all her stupid friends and she called out, 'Hey, little brother! Leila thinks you're really handsome.' She does it to tease me. One day I'm going to strangle her. I mean it."

Karim was no longer listening. He had noticed something else. His brother, the self-styled cool guy of Ramallah, was staring across at Violette with a soft, stupid look on his face. The very sight of it made Karim feel queasy.

He was about to dig Joni in the ribs and point out this odd new development when a roar came from down the hill. The soldiers were revving up the tanks' engines. They were about to roll back and take possession once more of the town.

"Mama! I've got to help Mama!" said Karim, suddenly remembering. "I'll call you."

His mother had already finished her shopping. She was struggling out onto the pavement, loaded with half a dozen bulging bags.

"Karim! There you are at last," she snapped. "Quick! They'll be here in a minute."

She had hardly finished speaking when, from below, they heard a crackle as the soldiers' loudspeaker cleared its throat and the awful, frightening rumble as the tanks came nearer and nearer up the hill.

"*Mamnou'a al tajwwol!*" the loudspeaker blared out. "Being outside is forbidden!"

"Hurry!" shouted Lamia. "Run!"

Together they scrambled home, over the litter of stones and rubble covering the street, clutching the flimsy plastic handles on their supermarket bags, hoping that they would hold until they and their food supplies were safely back inside.

Chapter Three

It was another week before the tanks rolled away again from the middle of town and the daytime curfew was lifted. The tanks would come now only in the evening, staying all night, to withdraw each dawn.

Karim felt as if a stone had been pressing down on his head and it had been eased off for a moment, as if he'd been a fly buzzing against a glass pane and the window had suddenly opened, as if he'd been an animal caught in a trap and the door had been left ajar so that he could squeeze out, at last, into the open air.

"I don't know what you're so cheerful about," Jamal said sourly. "They'll come back any time they like. They're playing with us. They're the cats and we're the mice."

Karim didn't bother to answer. He was hunting under his bed for his soccer ball. The moment had finally come when he could play his special game again. He'd wanted it more than anything else, more even than seeing Joni.

It was midday when the soldiers left. Hassan Aboudi, wearing his grey work suit, left the apartment at once, a worried frown on his face, to check on how his shop had fared during the long days of the curfew. There were reports that shells from Israeli tanks had damaged parts of the town center and whole buildings had been demolished. Jamal had locked himself in the bathroom with his razor and his hair gel. Lamia was gathering up her money and her bags, ready to go shopping.

"Fresh milk for you tomorrow, my love," she was saying to Sireen. "We'll have you well again soon."

Farah had been with Rasha since soon after breakfast. Karim could hear them giggling together out on the stairs.

With his ball under his arm, he tiptoed towards the front door, moving gingerly, holding his breath in case his mother called him back for some dull chore. He made it, turned the handle silently, opened the door, and slipped out.

Fifteen seconds later, he had bounded down the five flights of stairs and had doubled around behind the apartments, his whole body flexing itself like a spring that had been coiled up and had suddenly been released, his feet itching for the feel of the ball.

There was nobody around as far as he could see, and that was the way he wanted it. This was his time. He could play as he liked, on his own, with no one to watch or criticize.

He started at once. Kick, bounce, catch-ball-on-end-of-foot, kick, bounce....

He was well into it now, the rhythm possessing him, his mind emptying itself cleanly of the tension.

"Freedom," he was whispering to himself. "Freedom."

And then, above his head, a window opened in the wall and a scratchy, rasping voice yelled out, "Shut that noise up, will you? Can't an old man get any peace around here? If I hear that ball of yours banging on the wall again, I'll tell your father."

The window slammed shut again.

Karim wanted to shout and shake his fist at old Abu Ramzi, to kick his ball up high and smash his dirty windows. He didn't dare.

"I don't care if you like him or not," his father had often growled. "I don't like the man much myself. He's selfish and cantankerous, I grant you. But he's our neighbor. He's old and he deserves respect, and if I hear that you boys have been rude to him I will be extremely angry."

Karim picked up his ball and bounced it around in his hands, cursing under his breath, then he put it down and punched out with his fists, imagining with each strike that he was connecting with Abu Ramzi's ugly, angry face.

Suddenly he stopped. Someone behind him was laughing. He turned around, hot with embarrassment, and saw a boy.

The boy was perched on a pile of stones, grinning. He was taller than Karim, but thinner, and a little older—thirteen, perhaps. His T-shirt, which must once have been white, was now a pale grey, and the bottoms of his jeans were worn and frayed. There was something wild, something carefree, in the way he sat straddling the stones and looked down at Karim, his chipped front tooth showing as he laughed.

"Who do you think you're laughing at, huh?" said Karim, ready to be offended. The boy was vaguely familiar. He'd seen him around, in the grade above him at school. He didn't know his name.

The boy pointed up at the window.

"I'm laughing at him. And you."

But his smile was so friendly that Karim couldn't feel insulted after all.

The boy scrambled down off the stones.

"Want a game of soccer? I'll play with you."

"I can't. Didn't you hear him? He'll get me into trouble with my father."

At the word "father" a funny look crossed the boy's face.

He despises me, thought Karim.

The boy's expression shifted subtly. There was no contempt in it after all, but something more like envy.

They looked at each other silently for a moment, then the boy jerked his head towards the road.

"I know a better place than this. Want to come with me? We could play a good game there."

The voices of Karim's parents started up inside his head.

Don't be silly, Karim, he could hear his father say. *You don't know anything about this boy. He looks like the sort to get you into all kinds of trouble.*

Now his mother was chiming in.

What am I always telling you about rough kids? You want to pick up nasty habits? Or diseases? Then just go ahead.

Deliberately he ignored them. He bent down, scooped up his soccer ball and passed it to the boy.

"All right," he said. "As long as it's not too far. I'll come."

Chapter Four

Karim felt nervous as the boy walked quickly ahead, leading him further and further away from the familiar streets near his home. He'd never been this far on his own before, and certainly not to this part of town.

They had come over the crest of the hill and were now looking down into the sprawl of the refugee camp. Karim's uneasiness increased. The people in the refugee camp had lived in Ramallah since long before he, or even his parents, had been born. More than half a century ago, they'd been driven out of their old homes when the state of Israel had first been created. They were Palestinians, just as he was. But they kept to themselves.

"Packed in like sardines—most of them out of work," Karim remembered Lamia saying. "They're from the other side of Palestine. We don't know much about them really. You can't help feeling sorry for them, when you know what they've been through, but still, not the sort of people you want your kids to mix with, exactly. I mean.... "

She'd let the rest of the sentence dangle, with a frown of disapproval.

I hope no one sees me down here, Karim thought, looking over his shoulder. If Mama finds out, she'll go crazy.

Few people were around. Come to think of it, no one he knew was likely to come here. He began to breathe more easily.

"You live down there, huh?" he said, pointing towards the hap-

hazard warren of densely packed houses built of grey cement blocks, with narrow little lanes running crookedly between them, which made up the camp.

"Na. Over there. We moved out last year."

He nodded towards some open ground above the camp, where a little one-story house, built of cream-colored stone, sat in a patch of open ground, under the shade of a fig tree. It looked like a village farm, a leftover from a former age. It must have been there for centuries, long before the town had grown up all around it.

Karim thought the boy was moving towards the house, but instead he veered off sideways, and climbed up and over a tumbledown wall. Karim scrambled after him.

"Is this it?" he said.

"Yes. This is it."

The place could be good, Karim could see that at once. It was a section of flat open ground, nearly as big as a real soccer field. An old stone wall, built against the side of the hill, blocked one end. No trees, or anything else, were growing, except for some dried-up stalks of grass left over from the heat of summer. All along one side, running the whole length of the place, was a huge mass of rubble, the remains of a long row of demolished buildings. It was sixty-five feet wide and at least six and a half feet high, and it rose and dipped like a mountain range in a series of ridges and peaks. More rubbish had been dumped on top of it, and stones, chunks of concrete, old oil drums, sections of drainpipe and debris of all kinds had rolled down to litter the flat area below. The boy still had Karim's ball in his hands. He was bouncing it off his knees and catching it again.

"Here," he said suddenly, throwing the ball.

Karim leapt for it, foot outstretched, but tripped over a stone and fell, whacking his elbow on the ground.

It hurt so much that for a moment he couldn't move or speak. He lay on the ground, stunned, nursing his left arm in his right hand, wondering if the bone was smashed.

"Try straightening it out," the boy said, looking down at him anxiously.

Karim gritted his teeth and tried. He found he could stretch it after all, and the pain was going away already.

"It must be OK, then," the boy said, sounding relieved.

"It's these stones." Karim was struggling to his feet. "There's no space to play a real game. We'll fall over all the time."

The boy shrugged his thin shoulders and looked away.

He thinks I'm soft, thought Karim, so he picked up the ball and kicked it to him.

They tried to play for a while, dodging around, passing the ball to each other, hopping over the stones as they ran for it, but the boy stubbed his toes and Karim nearly twisted his ankle, so after a while, in silent consent, they gave up.

"It's lousy here after all," the boy said. "Sorry."

They were now up near the wall at the far end of the ground. Karim studied it. It wasn't anywhere near as good as the old wall at his apartment building, where the stone facing was perfectly smooth and regular. This wall was made of rough jutting boulders and was pitted with big holes where the cement had weakened and stones had fallen out.

At least it's a wall, Karim said to himself. It might do for my special game. The ball would just bounce funny, that's all.

It would be more fun, too, if the boy could join in and they could play together.

"It's not too bad up at this end." He kicked a couple of the smaller stones out of the way. "We could clear some of this lot and make a bit of space."

The boy didn't bother to answer. He was already lifting one of the boulders and staggering across to the edge of the ground, where there was a pile of stones from a broken-down wall. Karim could see that it was too heavy for him. The muscles of his thin arms were trembling under the strain and his face was going red.

His pride aroused, Karim looked around for an even bigger stone. He found one and tried to lift it, but his bruised elbow hurt too much and he dropped it again. To save face, he started picking up smaller stones and throwing them onto the pile.

The boy copied him. They were making a game of it now. They went faster and faster, collecting stones and hurling them off to the side.

"Whee! Bang! Gotcha!" the boy started shouting. "Right on the gun turret! One soldier down! Three to go!"

The pile of stones had become an Israeli tank in both their minds and they were letting them have it, seeing the enemy before their eyes with their helmets and body armor and rifles, daring them with nothing but their courage and the stones in their bare hands.

They stopped suddenly, out of breath, and looked around. Almost without realizing it, they'd cleared a good patch of ground. There was enough room now to play against the wall.

Karim didn't bother to explain his game. He simply started kicking the ball against the wall and the boy joined in. The rhythm came at once: kick, bounce, catch-the-ball-on-end-of-foot, kick, bounce....

It was good.

He's the best ever at this, thought Karim. Better than Joni, even as good as me.

He could have gone on for hours and hours, playing ball against that wall with him.

And then, from the mosque below the refugee camp, the words of the evening prayer sounded out across the city.

"Allahu akbar! Allahu akbar!
Ashhadu an la illaha illa Allah hay ala asalah!"

"It's late! I've got to go before the tanks come back. She'll kill me," Karim said, grabbing the ball and getting ready to run.

He was already dashing across the open space towards the road when he realized that the boy was still standing beside the wall.

"Hey!" he called back to him. "What's your name?"

The boy hesitated.

"Everyone calls me the Grasshopper. Just Hopper, usually. What's yours?"

Karim wished he had a cool nickname too.

"Karim," he said. "Karim Aboudi. See you again maybe."

"How about tomorrow?" The boy said it quickly, eagerly.

"OK. If the curfew's still off, I'll come back again then."

Chapter Five

Hassan Aboudi was in a fierce mood that evening, when the tanks had chased everyone inside once more. He walked around the apartment, picking things up and slamming them down again, kicking savagely at anything left lying on the floor. Karim sat motionless at the table, pretending to do some work. Farah had been twirling around in a frilly orange skirt she'd borrowed from Rasha, saying, "Look at me! What do you think? I'm prettier than Rasha, aren't I?" But she caught her father's eye and went tiptoeing off behind the sofa with her doll. Sireen, her ear infection a little better now, was sleeping peacefully in the girls' bedroom.

Lamia shot sideways glances at her husband as she stood at the ironing board.

"Everyone's in the same boat," she said to him at last. "All the other shopkeepers are having just as bad a time."

She might as well have thrown gas onto a fire, thought Karim, watching his father's face go red as he banged his fist down on the table, making the pencils rattle and roll around.

"What do you know about it?" he shouted. "I'm not like the other shopkeepers! Don't you understand anything? Nobody wants electrical goods at a time like this. 'Oh,' you think they're all saying, 'why don't we go along to Hassan Aboudi's shop and treat ourselves to a new TV, or one of those nice new irons, with all the money we've been earning while we've been locked down under curfew.' That's what they're saying, is it? Is it? In the same boat as George Boutros in his supermarket, with his queues of customers stretching away down the street every time their fridges empty out? Like the pharmacy, which sells out of everything as soon as they lift the curfew?"

Everyone looked at him, stunned. Hassan was normally a quiet man. His children had never heard such an outburst from him before.

He sat down on the sofa and put his head in his hands.

"I went down and opened up the shop today," he said in a quieter voice. "I looked around at all my stock and, I tell you, it broke my heart. Everything's covered in grit and dust. It looks terrible. Neglected. Unsellable. All the years I've been building the business up—all the work I've put in.... Do you know what I sold today? Batteries. Nothing but batteries. It's the only thing people want. How are we going to live on the sale of batteries? We'll be ruined if it goes on like this."

His voice was shaking. For one terrible moment, Karim was afraid that his father was going to cry. The idea of it made his skin crawl with embarrassment.

Lamia had been standing as if frozen, holding the iron up in the air, but now she put it back on its stand. She went over to the sofa and sat down beside her husband.

"It can't go on forever, *habibi*. It can't be as bad as this forever."

"Can't it? Why not?" said Hassan. "This occupation started when I was ten years old. Every year you think to yourself, it can't get any worse. And then it does. It does. Much worse. I tell you, the Israelis won't be happy until they've driven us all out and grabbed every inch of Palestine for themselves."

Karim breathed a sigh of relief. His father was off on his usual tack now. With a bit of luck he'd carry on in the same old groove, cursing the Israelis and the occupation, getting away from the personal stuff.

"Anyway," said Lamia, "there's always my salary from the university to tide us over."

She saw at once that she'd made a mistake. Karim could tell that by the way she bit her lip. Hassan dropped her hand, which he'd been holding, and gave a bitter little laugh.

"Oh, that's just great. I'm the sort of man who lives off his wife now, am I? And we're the sort of family that makes do on one part-time secretary's salary. Isn't that just great?"

Jamal had appeared at the door of the boys' bedroom. He caught Karim's eye and flicked his head sideways, beckoning him to come. Gratefully, Karim slipped off his chair and sidled around the sofa.

Jamal shut the door behind them.

"Better leave them alone," he said.

"What did he mean, we'll be ruined?"

"Don't ask me. I'm not a businessman. I'm never going to be, either. Nothing but worry all the time. Unless you call sound engineers businessmen."

Karim bit back the automatic retort that he had nearly blurted out, the usual kind of crack about people who fantasize about having amazingly cool careers as sound engineers and managers of top rock bands, but are really sad losers and pimple-heads. He was glad he hadn't said anything. For once, it was good that Jamal was there, that he had an older brother who had bothered to get him out of the room, away from embarrassing scenes.

"Did you go past school when you went out?" Jamal said.

"No. Why?"

"Because the Israelis have occupied it since the last curfew break. They've had their tanks parked all over the soccer field and they've smashed down the walls. They've wrecked the labs and the classrooms and stolen all the computers. We won't be able to go back for ages."

Karim bunched his fists. However much he hated school, he

was enraged at the idea of the enemy crawling all over it, their tank tracks churning up the soccer field. But then he thought, at least I'll be having a holiday for a while. That means I can go back to our special place and play soccer with Hopper.

Jamal was giving him a funny look.

"When are you seeing Joni again?"

"I don't know. Soon. Tomorrow. The next day. Why?"

Jamal was shuffling his feet around on the rug, studying his shoes as if he'd never seen them before.

"Look, Karim, you're my brother, right?"

"You've only just discovered that? After twelve years?"

"We're good friends, aren't we?"

Karim frowned, instantly suspicious. With this build-up, Jamal must want something big.

"Up to a point," he said cautiously.

"I know I was rude about your soccer abilities, but I didn't mean it. I think you do great headers. Honestly."

"Yeah, all right. Get on with it. What do you want?"

Jamal licked his lips.

"You've got to promise, on the holy Koran, that you won't tell anyone."

"I'll think about it."

"No, promise me now."

"Come on, Jamal. Who do you think I am? Mr. Number One World's Biggest Sucker? You've got to tell me what it is first."

"Yeah, I suppose so. Fair enough. OK."

Jamal took a deep breath.

"I want you to persuade Joni to get ahold of a photo of Violette for me. Without her knowing," he blurted out.

Karim stared at him, too astonished to even laugh. He might fight with Jamal, he might mock him and insult him and try to get the better of him in every way he could, but Jamal was still his older brother. He was still someone Karim secretly admired, whose good opinion he valued more than anyone else's. How could he have gone soft in the head from one day to the next? And to think that it was all on account of Violette Boutros, a girl he'd known all his life, who'd changed, admittedly, but only into the giggliest, stupidest fluff-head (according to Joni) in the whole of Palestine! Or the Middle East, come to think of it.

"You're kidding," he said at last.

"I'm not."

"You've got to be. Violette? That Barbie doll? She's... "

Jamal had moved before Karim had even blinked, and Karim's head was locked under Jamal's arm. Laughter was trying to bubble out of Karim. He thought for one breathless moment that he would suffocate and he pushed Jamal off with a superhuman heave.

"What'll you give me if I agree?" he managed to gasp.

Jamal's eyes narrowed. The brothers were on familiar ground now, bargaining.

"Well, for a start, I won't tell Mama I saw you go off with that scruffy kid this afternoon. Down towards the refugee camp."

Karim stared at him, horrified.

"You didn't see me with anyone," he blustered. "And if you did, it must have been someone else."

"Think I don't know my own brother? It was you. Who is he?"

"Just someone. Anyway, what were you doing down there yourself?"

"None of your business."

It was a stalemate. They looked at each other. Karim was the first to give way. A strange feeling had come over him, a sudden surge of affection for Jamal. Inexplicably he wanted to please him. He didn't even want to bargain anymore, even though it meant giving away the best advantage he would have for a long, long time.

"OK, I'll do it," he said.

He had taken his brother by surprise. Jamal's brows shot up so high they disappeared into his hairline.

"What, for nothing?"

"Yes, you great soft lover boy."

"Wow, Karim, you're a good kid. You really are. Total secrecy, all right? Lips buttoned. And Joni's too. You'll have to make up some kind of story to tell him."

"Yeah, well, you leave Joni to me."

Karim felt grand and lordly and generous.

"Jamal! Karim!" their mother called out from the kitchen. "Come and eat."

Karim had been afraid that supper that night would be tense, his parents tight-lipped and irritable and the little girls whining and cross, but to his surprise his father looked almost cheerful as he served the meat onto their plates.

"I hear your school's out of commission, boys," he said. "It's a shocking mess, so I'm told."

Jamal and Karim nodded.

"So you're going to have a few days off. Well, I want you to pack a bag each tonight. We're going to Deir Aldalab to see your grand mother. She called today to tell me that the olives are ready to pick. Anyway, it's been months since we made it down to the farm."

Karim looked sideways at Jamal. As he expected, Jamal looked horrified.

"But surely you can't leave the shop, Baba?" he said. "I thought.... Doesn't it need...I could help you straighten things out if you like?"

Hassan said nothing, but a heavy frown settled back on his forehead.

"There's more to be gained by getting in the olive harvest," Lamia said quickly. "Your father ordered new stock for the shop a while ago. He'll open up again once it's delivered and things have calmed down."

"We'll leave early," said Hassan. "I want you up and ready by seven thirty."

"But..." began Jamal.

Karim kicked him under the table. Jamal glared at him, but said no more.

Farah was looking excited.

"Can Rasha come, Baba? Please. Ple-e-ase!" she whined.

"No, *habibti*," said her father. "It'll be too much for your grandma."

Karim looked down at his plate. He had loved going to the village when he was Farah's age, especially when Joni was there. It was in the village, in fact, that they'd first become friends. Their fathers had grown up there together, going to the village school and playing all day out in the olive groves, as close throughout their youth as Karim and Joni were now, in spite of the fact that Karim's family was Muslim and Joni's Christian.

I wouldn't mind if Joni was coming too, Karim thought, scooping up a spoonful of beans.

But Joni wouldn't be going to the village, he was sure of that. Joni's Greek Orthodox school had been left untouched by the occupying army, this time at least. Joni and Violette would be going back to school tomorrow, their bags weighted down with books.

I'll think of something, thought Karim. I'll work out an excuse so that they leave me behind.

Chapter Six

I t was already nine in the morning when they left Ramallah at last. Karim sat in the back of the car, hugging the corner, keeping as far away from Farah as he could, disgusted with himself, his family, and the world in general.

He had spent hours after supper working out one good reason after another why he should be allowed to stay at home, but when at last he'd plucked up the courage to tackle his father, he found that Jamal had got there first.

"I've said Jamal doesn't have to come, but I'm not leaving both of you here," Hassan said irritably. "The whole point of Jamal staying behind is so that he can catch up with his studies in peace and quiet. If you're here too, you'll end up bickering all day long. No, that's enough, Karim. No pulled faces please. If you're so desperate to study, you can take your books down to the village. Have you packed your things yet? Why not? Go and do it now."

Days of boredom stretched ahead. There would be endless visits with relatives. He would have to endure hours of nothing, sitting respectfully on uncomfortable chairs, as the adults lounged in the comfortable ones and talked on and on. He would have to put up with his uncles' heavy teasing, and his aunts' fond memories of all the cute things he'd done when he was a baby. His grandmother would stuff him with endless quantities of food that he wouldn't particularly want to eat. His cousins would try to involve him in their games at first, but they'd soon go off with the other village boys and he'd be left alone to watch Farah and Sireen being revoltingly petted and spoiled by everyone.

The morning rush of traffic in the center of Ramallah was past its worst, but the narrow streets were still choked with cars, vans, and taxis. Drivers were irritable and impatient as they tried to resume their normal lives after weeks of inactivity. Everyone was in a hurry, desperate to get their goods to the market or to restock their empty shelves.

A minibus crowded with people pulled out suddenly in front of Hassan's car and tried to overtake a man pushing a handcart laden with oranges. It blocked the oncoming traffic and everything lurched to a halt.

"Go on, my darling, no problem. Push in front of everyone if you like. Just don't let me catch you out on your own after dark," Hassan said sarcastically to the inside of the windshield.

Farah, playing with her doll, leaned it up against Karim's arm. He jerked away and turned his head to look sideways out the window, wishing he could simply open the car door and jump out.

The traffic was really stuck now. Horns blared. Drivers shouted and gesticulated.

Someone appeared at the window of the front passenger seat, which Lamia had opened to let in some air.

"Verses for sale," said a wheedling voice. "From the holy Koran. Give what you like."

Karim sat up with a jerk. He knew that voice. He leaned forward to look.

Too late, he saw that it belonged to Hopper. He shrank back into his corner again, but Hopper had seen him.

"Oh, hi, Karim," he said breezily, dropping his salesman's tone. "Where are you going? I thought we were meeting up today?"

"Can't," mumbled Karim. "We're going to our village. Don't know when we'll be back."

Lamia had been fumbling in her purse. She pulled out a few

coins and dropped them into Hopper's palm. He handed her a little piece of paper inscribed with verses and leaned into the car to talk to Karim.

At that moment, to Karim's intense relief, the traffic ahead thinned and the car jerked forward. Looking back, Karim could see Hopper standing on the pavement, waving at him, a friendly smile on his face. He raised his hand and moved it sideways in a surreptitious answering signal, then subsided into his corner again.

"Who on earth was that?" said his mother disapprovingly.

"Just someone. He goes to my school. I don't know him really."

He was aware of Farah's bright eyes inquisitively studying his face. He nudged her sharply with his elbow.

"What are you staring at?" he hissed at her.

He picked up her doll, which she had propped against him again, and threw it into the opposite corner.

"Mama, Karim's being nasty to me," whined Farah.

Lamia wasn't listening.

"Selling Koranic verses like that," she said. "It's no more or less than begging."

"What else can people do when their livelihoods have gone?" said Hassan, accelerating as the open road stretched ahead. "May God be merciful to them, poor souls."

In the past, it had taken no more than half an hour to drive to the village. It had been a frequent outing on a Friday, the one-day weekend, when schools and businesses were closed. Since the latest unrest, though, the journey had become difficult and unpredictable. A deep trench had been cut right through the main road, making it impassable, and a new, heavily guarded road, which only Israelis were allowed to use, had sliced across the countryside, cutting old country roads in half.

Hassan had spent an hour the previous evening calling relatives for the latest news on roadblocks, so that he could plan the best route.

"Two hours if we're lucky," he grunted, as they began to leave the new sprawl of Ramallah behind.

Karim had never before ridden along the tortuous little country lanes, which meandered from one village to the next, climbing the steep rocky hillsides and plunging down again into the valleys. He bothered, for a while, to notice what was passing outside the window, to look at the new houses on the outskirts of each village and wonder about the burned-out cars along the side of the road. Then he lost interest and stared unseeingly at the sky.

"Look at this," Hassan said with satisfaction when an hour had passed. "We're doing well. Half an hour at the most from here, I reckon. Call my mother, Lamia. Tell her we'll be there soon."

Lamia reached down into her handbag to pull out her cell phone. She was holding it in her hand, ready to punch in the number, when it rang. She held it to her ear and listened for a moment.

"It's your sister," she said. "She's heard that there's trouble ahead." She handed the phone to her husband.

He listened too, asked a couple of questions, tutted with exasperation, and handed the mobile back to her.

"We'll have to go back and find another way around," he said, slowing down as they approached a corner. "I'll turn at the next opportunity."

"What is it? What's happened?" asked Karim.

"There's been an incident," his mother said over her shoulder. "Israeli settlers attacked a village last night. Three Palestinians killed and one settler wounded. The soldiers have blocked the road and they're not letting anyone through."

They were around the corner now. Ahead of them, instead of the emptiness of the country road that they were expecting, was a line of cars and minibuses. Beyond it was a khaki armored vehicle, with a yellow light flashing on its roof.

The car slid to a halt. Hassan looked over his shoulder.

"Nothing coming up behind," he said. "It's narrow, but I'd better try and turn here. Looks like we'll be stuck for hours if we don't go back."

He began to reverse up the road.

A sudden violent hammering on the roof of the car made everyone inside jump with fright. Karim felt his hair stand on end and he gripped the headrest of his mother's seat in front. Then he heard shouts. Through the square of the car window he could see only the chest of the soldier who was standing beside it, the body armor, which covered his upper half, and the rifle he was gripping in his arms.

Another soldier had appeared beside his father's window.

"Move up," he said in thickly accented Arabic, pointing to the line of cars in front.

Hassan drove forward to park behind the last car in the line. The soldiers had walked alongside. Now one of them wrenched open the driver's door.

"Get out," he said to Hassan.

The other soldier rapped on the front passenger window to make Lamia open it. He bent down to scrutinize everyone in the car, peering out from under the rim of his heavy steel helmet, his eyes darting nervously towards Karim and away again.

"How old is he?" he said to Lamia, jerking his head to indicate Karim.

"Eleven," Lamia said, looking straight ahead.

Karim opened his mouth to say, "Excuse me. I'm twelve," but he shut it again.

He could now see the line of men and boys, some only a little older than himself, who had been ordered out of their cars and were standing at the side of the road, guarded by a soldier, who stood in front of them, his finger on the trigger of his gun.

The soldier pulled his head back out of the car.

"Shut the window," he said. "Shut all the windows. Stay in the car."

Wordlessly, Lamia obeyed. From the stiff way she held her head, Karim could imagine her face. It would be quite expressionless. She would be refusing, with all her self-control, to give the soldier the satisfaction of seeing her fear and anger.

The soldier had disappeared now, running back up the road to deal with the next car that had appeared. Karim leaned forward between the front seats.

"What are they going to do with Baba, Mama?"

"How should I know? You think I understand these animals?"

Farah had grabbed her doll when the soldier's face had appeared at the window of the car. She was holding it against her chest, crooning to it. Sireen seemed unconscious of the tension around her. She had scrambled into the empty driver's seat and was standing at the steering wheel, pretending to drive the car.

Karim was watching the line of Palestinian men and boys. Their guard was shouting something he couldn't hear and waving his gun at them. The men were shuffling uneasily and looking at the ground. Some were fumbling with the buttons of their shirts. The soldier jabbed the long barrel of his rifle at the nearest man and shouted again. The men began to move more quickly.

Karim craned forward to look.

"What are they doing?"

Farah's thumb had been stuck in her mouth. She took it out.

"Why is Baba taking off his clothes?" she said.

Lamia didn't answer. She had pulled Sireen into her arms and was holding her close. Sireen was struggling to get away.

The men had stripped to the waist now. Their shirts and jackets lay in heaps on the ground. The soldiers kicked at them and shouted again.

"I don't believe it," moaned Lamia. "To humiliate them. Old men, too. In front of their families, and strangers."

Slowly, the men were undoing belts, buttons, and zippers, letting their trousers slip to the ground, taking off shoes and socks.

Karim watched in horrified fascination. Giggles of embarrassment were bubbling up inside him. The men, standing out in the road in their underpants, looked funny and pathetic, helpless and stupid. They were staring at the ground, at the sky, into the distance, anywhere except at each other, or at the waiting line of cars in which their women and children sat, witnesses to their shame.

I didn't know Baba's legs were so thin, Karim thought, or that his shoulders were so round.

He couldn't bear to look at his father. He couldn't look away.

An old man, who until a few minutes before had been a dignified figure in the long robe and white headdress that elderly men in the village usually wore, was standing beside Hassan. Almost naked, stripped of everything, he was trying to stand upright, to hold up his head and show, in his face at least, the dignity which had been taken from him. As Karim watched, the old man staggered. Hassan put out his hand to steady him. The old man leaned on him gratefully, and as they stood together, Hassan began to gently pat the old man's hand.

Even from this distance, Karim could see that it was violently trembling.

His desire to laugh had gone. He couldn't believe that he'd felt it at all.

It's what they want, he thought. To make us look silly.

There was a burning pain inside him. He'd never thought much about his father before. Sometimes he'd been scared when Hassan had been angry. Sometimes he'd glowed when he'd praised him. He'd always assumed that his father knew best, that his decisions were right, that he could protect his family and would always be there to give advice, that he would know what was right and what was wrong.

All those sure things shifted in his mind as he saw his father's humiliation. Hot, red anger pulsed behind his eyes.

He came to with a start at the sound of a click. Sireen had wriggled off Lamia's lap and was back in the driver's seat. She had opened the door and was jumping out onto the road.

"No!" shouted Karim. "Sireen! Come back!"

Without stopping to think, he opened his own door and ran to pick her up. He heard a shout and before he could reach her was pulled up short by a soldier grabbing his arm.

"What are you doing, Palestinian?" the soldier snarled at him.

"My sister," babbled Karim. "She's only four. She opened the door herself. I... "

Sireen had run back and grabbed hold of his leg. With the other hand she pulled at the soldier's grey-green uniform trousers.

"Please, uncle," she said. "I want my Baba."

The young soldier looked down at her, as if he didn't understand. He hesitated, seemingly disconcerted at the touch of the little girl's hand. Karim could feel that the soldier's fingers, still gripping his arm, were shaking.

He's terrified, he thought, with surprise. He thinks we're going to attack him.

He could almost smell the soldier's fear.

"She didn't mean any harm," he said, hating the placating note he could hear in his own voice. "I'll take her back to the car."

The soldier shoved at him roughly.

"Take her. If there's any more trouble from you, you go over there and join the other terrorists."

Karim scooped Sireen up in his arms and ran back to the car with her.

Lamia had half opened the door, but another soldier was alongside the car now, ordering her to shut it. Karim handed Sireen to her and jumped into the back seat.

"Oh, my darling," sobbed Lamia, her face in Sireen's hair.

Karim was trembling violently. He felt sick with the backwash of fear.

Farah moved across and leaned against him, her thumb firmly

in her mouth. Her other hand clutched at his arm. This time, he didn't push her away.

I hate them. I hate them. I hate them, he thought, unable now to look at his father, who still stood, reduced to an object of ridicule, beside the bewildered old man.

Chapter Seven

They came into the village at last, driving past the half-built houses on the outskirts, and the old school, and the souvenir factory, closed since the present troubles had begun. Hassan Aboudi had been allowed to dress himself and return to his car at the end of an agonizing hour. He had bent his head over the steering wheel for a long moment, gripping it so hard that his knuckles had whitened. Karim hadn't been able to see his father's face, and he was glad. His own face was burning with embarrassment and shame.

I'd have fought back, he told himself savagely. I wouldn't ever let them do that to me.

But he knew that his father had had no choice. He knew he'd have been forced to bear it too.

No one had said a word for the last half-hour of the journey. Lamia had tried once to put her hand on her husband's arm, but he had shaken it off roughly. Even Sireen, who usually babbled nonsense to herself, sat in passive silence.

It was a relief to arrive at last at the old family home. Karim's grandmother came to the door, wiping her hands on a towel. She was wearing, as she always did, traditional clothes: a richly embroidered black dress that fell to the floor and was belted round her wide waist, and a dazzlingly white scarf that covered her hair.

Karim expected Farah to run towards her, as she normally did, stretching out her doll to show her grandmother, anxious to get the first hug ahead of Sireen, but to his surprise she held back and let Sireen go on ahead.

He looked away, down the hill. His great-uncle, Abu Feisal, was coming up the path from the olive terraces below, his pruning knife still in his hand. The old man's face was split in a smile of welcome, but Karim could hardly bear to look at him. He kept remembering that other old man at the side of the road, with his long grey robe and undergarments lying around his feet.

"I thought you'd never get here," his grandmother, Um Hassan, was saying, as she disentangled herself from Sireen and led the way inside. "Held you up all that time, did they? It's getting worse and worse. Trouble, trouble, all the time."

It was the smell of the old house more than anything that struck Karim every time he came. The slight mustiness, the whiff of wood smoke, the lingering wealth of his grandmother's cooking, the warmth of new bread, the tang of lemons, the spiciness of drying herbs—without even being aware of them, the rich mixture usually reduced him to childhood again, and somehow relaxed him.

Today, though, he didn't like it. Everything disgusted him today.

News of their arrival had spread and relatives from nearby houses were arriving. Large great-aunts with loud country voices shrieked out greetings. Small grandchildren clung to their floor-length skirts and stared with round-eyed shyness at Farah and Sireen.

"Well, Karim, so you're here," his grandmother said with a comfortable nod. "Ahmed and Latif are at school. They're looking forward to seeing you. Remember how all you cousins used to play down at the stream?"

Karim smiled awkwardly. He hadn't been to the stream for years. The thought of those childish games was mortifying.

The afternoon slipped past. Lamia whispered an account of Hassan's ordeal to his relatives. They tutted over it and talked quickly of other things. News was passed on. Several people in the village had died since they had last been here. A number of babies had been born. A new, radical sheikh had come to the mosque. The old church had been hit by a tank shell.

A whole hillside just outside the village had been confiscated two years earlier to make a big new settlement for Israelis, a move which had enraged everyone for miles around. There were always goings-on to report from there. This time, it was an attack on the settlement by three young Palestinian men, who had hurled stones and petrol bombs at a car on the settlers' road and had been taken off to prison in Israel.

"We'll think about picking the olives tomorrow," Um Hassan said as she served up the meal she had hastily prepared. "Let's forget all our troubles this evening. The family's together for once. That's the main thing."

"Are you expecting problems from the settlers, Mother, when we go out to pick?" Karim heard his father say.

"We thought there would be last week, when we went over to the far side," his grandmother replied. "But there wasn't, thank God. Things have been quiet up there recently. We should be all right, *inshallah*. Best keep a careful lookout, all the same."

That night, for the first time since her babyhood, Farah wet her bed. She tried to hide the sodden sheets, but her grandmother, finding them, washed them and hung them outside, and put the mattress out to air. No one scolded her. No one needed to. Farah was deeply ashamed.

It was chilly in the early morning air. The heat of summer was well past now. A cold November wind rattled the shutters and blew dead leaves around the terrace at the back of the house. Karim would have liked to snuggle down into his bed and sleep in, but his father came into the bedroom he was sharing with the girls and shook him awake. When he went yawning into the kitchen in

51

search of breakfast, the baskets ready for the olives were stacked by the door and Um Hassan was busy packing up bundles of food and bottles of water for the pickers to take out with them. She would be staying at home, minding the little girls and preparing a lavish meal for the evening.

The family had already harvested the olives from the terraces near the village but they still had to tackle the more distant trees. The land, which Karim's great-grandfather had inherited from his father, was now jointly owned by a wide network of relations. They banded together when the work had to be done—weeding, pruning, repairs to old terrace walls, and the picking itself.

The hillside where they planned to work today was nearly two miles away. Hassan was loading up the car when Karim went outside the house. He had piled the baskets in the back and was attaching ladders to the roof.

"Come on. Get in," he called to Lamia.

She squeezed into the back beside the baskets, and an aunt took the front seat.

"Karim and I are going to walk," the old great-uncle, Abu Feisal, said, clapping Karim on the shoulder with his gnarled, work-calloused hand. "We'll see you there."

They set off down the village street towards the entrance to the lane that wound between old stone walls into the valley and up the hill on the other side.

Karim had always liked his uncle Abu Feisal. When he was little, Abu Feisal had taken him out sometimes into the countryside, showing him where the best prickly pear fruits grew and warning him of the places where snakes liked to bask. Today, though, he felt tongue-tied as they set out from the house together.

He was glad, at least, that his cousins had had to go to school. They seemed to have grown out of all the things they used to share. Ahmed and Latif had no computer, so he couldn't talk to them about his favorite games. They'd tried to interest him last night in their father's new horse. He'd gone to look at it in its stable, but there hadn't been much to say.

It was warmer now that the sun was up, though a chill breeze was blowing, ruffling the slim silver-green leaves of the old olive trees on each side of the lane. Abu Feisal didn't seem to mind Karim's silence. He was content to say nothing much himself, merely pointing out a brightly colored bird from time to time, or reminding Karim of the day they'd picked blackberries from the clump at the bottom of the hill.

The old man walked fast. Karim, still unfit after the long days of curfew in Ramallah, was out of breath as he tried to keep abreast with him up the steep hill.

They came to the top at last. Karim had been looking down at his feet for the last few hundred feet, his mind far away in Ramallah, divided between Joni and Hopper. He looked up as they came over the rise and gasped.

It was years since he'd been this far from the village, but he'd been expecting the landscape to be as he'd always known it: the rounded stone-strewn hill beyond, on top of which flocks of sheep and goats used to graze, and the lower slopes ringed with olive terraces. Instead, not more than a half mile away, a high wall surrounded the crown of the hill. Outside it, creating a kind of no-man's-land, were two fences of barbed wire and rows of lights suspended from high poles. Inside the walls, white houses marched in regimented lines and a huge crane towered above a half-finished block of flats. The blue and white flag of Israel fluttered from the top.

His uncle had walked on, but he turned back when he saw that Karim had stopped, and nodded as he took in the surprise on the boy's face.

"Didn't you know that this had happened? Didn't you hear us talking about the new settlement here?"

"Yes, I suppose so." Karim hadn't listened closely to the talk about the settlement. "I didn't know it was so close."

He could see his father's car now. It was parked at the side of the road in the valley below. His parents and aunt were setting off with their baskets into the lowest terrace on the slope opposite the hill on which the settlement lay.

Karim and his uncle had just passed the car and were walking off the road, hurrying along the terrace between the olive trees to catch up with the others, when the first shot rang out. It hit a stone a few metres away from Karim and shattered it, sending sharp fragments in all directions. Karim was so scared that for a moment he couldn't move. He stood, petrified and confused, unable even to tell where the sound had come from.

His uncle recovered first.

"Quick! Get behind a tree!" he shouted, scrambling up the wall to the terrace above, where older trees with thicker trunks offered slightly better protection.

Karim started to follow, but then he heard a voice shouting in English, "Stop! Stop! Don't move!" and a second shot pinged on the terrace wall ahead.

Cautiously, he turned around. He could see men on the opposite hillside, running down from the high-walled settlement above. He counted them. Five.

Karim's mother was shouting to him now.

"Karim! Do what they say! Don't move!"

The settlers were running fast towards the olive pickers. They all carried guns. They stopped at the bottom of the hill, 150 feet or more away.

"What are you doing here?" one of them shouted, still in English. "Drop your weapons and get out."

Karim couldn't understand everything they said. From further along the terrace, he heard his father call back, "We don't have weapons. No arms. We come only to pick our olives."

One of the settlers laughed.

"*Your* olives? Forget it. This is part of the settlement now. You won't ever pick olives here again. You want to get shot? No? Then get out now."

Abu Feisal appeared from behind the tree where he had taken cover.

"This place," he called out bravely, "it is ours. We have the papers. My grandfather—"

The only answer was a bullet, which hit the tree eight inches from his hand.

"It's OK!" Lamia called out. "You don't need to shoot anymore. We're going."

"Keep your hands up!" one of the settlers shouted back. "Drop the baskets. Leave them. Go on—get out!"

"And you can tell your terrorist friends to keep away, you hear?" yelled another.

It seemed a long way back to the car, knowing that the settlers' rifles were still trained on their backs. Karim felt his shoulders twitch in frightened expectation as he turned away from them, sure that at any moment a bullet would sear into him. His instinct told him to run, but his brain told him not to make any sharp or sudden movements. He could hear his parents and aunt behind him now, his aunt's breath coming in panting gasps.

Without the baskets there was just enough room for the five of them in the car. Gingerly, Hassan turned it and began to drive as fast as he could up the hill towards the village. Tears were running down the old aunt's broad cheeks.

"Thieves! Thieves! I've come here to pick our olives every year since I could walk!"

A sharp crack from behind made them all flinch.

"Get down!" screamed Lamia. "They're still shooting!"

Hassan hunched over the wheel and pushed the accelerator down as far as it would go. The car bounded to the top of the hill.

He pulled up when they were safely over the crest.

"Did it hit? Is everyone all right?"

"It went into the bumper, I think," said Abu Feisal, twisting round to look out of the rear window. "Not into a tire anyway, thank God."

Karim discovered that he was shaking, convulsed in tremors from head to foot. He did his best to control them, taking deep breaths and clasping his hands tightly together. He didn't want the others to think he was afraid.

"How can they do it?" he burst out angrily. "Stop us from picking our own olives! On our own land! They've just stolen it! Why didn't anyone stop them?"

Abu Feisal laughed bitterly.

"We tried. Don't think we didn't. It was a shock. We had no idea they were coming. They arrived out of the blue—it was a Tuesday, I think—just four or five caravans and a bulldozer. Before we had any idea what was happening, they'd gone up the hill and had started bulldozing the ground. As soon as we realized what they were doing, we came running, everyone did, the whole village more or less. We got as close to them as we could, but they had guns and they shot at us. What could we do?"

Karim wanted to shout, "Something! You could have done something! Anything!" but he didn't want to seem rude. He wriggled his shoulders impatiently.

"Karim, you don't know what it was like." His aunt, who was squashed in beside him, patted his knee. "Some of us lay down on the road in front of the trucks and cement mixers. The settlers wouldn't stop for that. After they'd run over Abu Ali and broken both his legs, we knew they wouldn't care what they did to us. Our boys went out every day and threw stones at any settler who went past. Then the soldiers came with tanks and Jeeps. The boys threw stones and Molotov cocktails at them and the soldiers shot back. Didn't you hear about how Walid's boy was killed? He was fourteen. There's a memorial to him in the village. And his brother lost an eye. After that, when anyone tried to resist, they came to the village and arrested them, and took them off to jail in Israel. Three of your own cousins are still there."

"Yes, but those trees, that hill, it's ours! You said, Baba. You told me about how your great-grandfather...."

Hassan was negotiating the sharp corner by the mosque, where an old man was trying to load a sack onto the back of a donkey. He didn't say anything until he was safely past.

"We've done everything," he said resignedly. "I took the documents myself to show a lawyer. He's presented them in court to prove our ownership. That was two years ago. There's a case dragging on. It's costing us a fortune. And in the meantime the settlement's been built. How can anyone get them out now?"

"They must be planning to expand," said Abu Feisal heavily. "Why else would they have shot at us? They're planning to take the other hillside too. You'll see."

No one answered.

Chapter Eight

Sixteen people crowded around Um Hassan's table that evening to eat the huge meal that she had spent the day preparing. Lamia had joined aunts and cousins in the kitchen. They had stuffed zucchinis and eggplants with a spicy lamb filling, chopped vegetables, rolled meatballs, roasted chickens, stirred sauces, boiled mountains of rice and sprinkled fistfuls of garden herbs.

The steaming bowls and laden platters of delicious food that jostled for space on the flowery plastic tablecloth would normally have brought Karim hurrying to sit down, eager to start. Tonight, though, he hung back. He'd been miserable all afternoon, ever since they'd come back from the olive terraces.

Liberator of Palestine! he jeered at himself, remembering the list he'd written at home in Ramallah. I haven't even got the guts to stand up to a bunch of bullying Israeli settlers. I ran away at the first shot.

He'd sat outside the wall that surrounded his grandmother's vegetable patch for a long time, flicking pebbles at an old soda can abandoned under a lemon tree. Life was unpredictable and frightening in Ramallah, but the village, the crowd of relations, the sense of ownership of the old family lands, which had been there in the background of his life ever since he could remember, had always seemed fixed and unassailable.

Everything seemed shaky now. Nothing was permanent any

more. And what upset him most of all was that everyone was so calm and accepting. His mind kept turning back to his father.

He's weak. Weak! he thought, remembering with a shudder how Hassan Aboudi had stood, almost naked, under the contemptuous stare of the soldiers, and how he'd run like a frightened rabbit from the settlers' guns.

Karim took his place at last at the table, flushing angrily when his mother sent him off again to wash his hands, watching sourly while Farah and Sireen climbed on and off their father's knees. He avoided the eyes of his cousins, who were boasting about the stones they'd thrown a week ago, when a gang of settlers had come to the village in the night and had rampaged about, shooting holes in people's water tanks and cutting down the power lines.

He concentrated on picking out the butter-fried almonds that garnished the rice and putting them at the side of the plate. They were his favorite tidbit and he always saved them till last. In spite of himself, he couldn't help relishing his grandmother's wonderful food.

The two men nearest him, husbands of Abu Feisal's daughters, were talking about America now.

"I've been thinking it over for a long time," one was saying. "My brother's got a pharmacy in Boston. I could stay with him while I get started over there."

"It wouldn't be difficult for you," the other answered. "They always want people with math degrees. But look at me! Unemployed ex-manager of an ex-tourist hotel for ex-tourists, who aren't going to come back to this land for the foreseeable future. I've got no paper qualifications at all. You're right to think about it, though. Emigration's the only hope for us now. What does Ayesha think?"

"She doesn't want to go. Hates the idea of leaving her family. But I keep telling her the kids would have a better future in America. We're finished. Palestine's finished."

Karim usually ate his almonds slowly, crunching them pleasurably one by one. This time he shoveled them all up in a single spoonful, put them into his mouth, chewed hastily, and swallowed. Then he pushed his chair back and stood up. He couldn't bear the conversation any longer.

Farah and Sireen had already abandoned the table and were sitting on the sofa watching TV. Karim sat down in the far corner and stared unseeingly at the screen. A Syrian soap opera was on, a series he usually enjoyed. Tonight, though, it seemed unbearably stupid and pointless.

The program ended and the screen was filled by a whirling globe, heralding the news. The announcer looked down at his notes, then stared into the camera.

A suicide bomber detonated a massive bomb outside a café in Jerusalem this afternoon. Eleven Israelis were killed. Four of them were secondary-school students, relaxing after their exams. The bomber has not been named.

Something like triumph exploded in Karim's head.

"Yes!" he whispered. "*Yes!*"

The conversation at the table had stopped. The adults, some with spoons or forks halfway to their mouths, had stopped eating and had swivelled round in their chairs to look at the TV.

"What? What's happened?" said Lamia, who had been in the kitchen and was now emerging with another bowl of lamb and okra stew.

"A bombing operation," said Hassan quietly. "In Jerusalem. Eleven dead."

Lamia grunted and put the bowl down on the table.

"Where did the bomber come from? Did they say?"

"No, listen. He hasn't finished yet. Yes, there you are. Ramallah or Bethlehem. They're not sure yet."

"There'll be reprisals," said Lamia, shaking her head. "The tanks'll come back in. They'll probably bomb the refugee camps. We might not be able to get home."

"Not if he came from Bethlehem," said Hassan. "They'll catch the worst of it there. They'll find his family's home and bulldoze it, then they'll put the whole city back under curfew."

"Isn't your mother in Bethlehem?" Um Hassan turned to one of the brothers-in-law who had been discussing emigration.

"Yes." Looking worried, he had already reached for his cell phone. "I'll call her and remind her to stock up on her blood-pressure pills. Last time the tanks came in she ran out of them. She could easily have had a stroke."

Karim wanted to shout at everyone, "Didn't you hear what the man said? The guy sacrificed his own life! He was a hero—a martyr! He did something for all of us—for Palestine! Don't you care?" He got up off the sofa and went outside into the darkness. He'd never felt so angry and lonely before.

He heard a chair scrape back in the room behind him and was afraid that someone would come out and ask him what the matter was. To get away, he ran around the side of the house to the old storerooms at the back. No one would be likely to come here.

Too late, he realized that the light in one of the two storerooms was on and that someone was coming out. It was his uncle. Karim turned to slink back, out of the light, but Abu Feisal had seen him.

"Karim," he said. "It's you." He didn't sound at all surprised. "Come in here. I want to show you something."

Reluctantly, Karim followed his uncle into the storeroom. He'd hardly ever been in this old room, and never after dark. It was big and square. The vaulted ceiling, from which hung a single light bulb, rose to a high point. Niches in the stone walls held bottles of olives and drying onions. A bundle of kindling lay near the door and in the center of the room, lipping over a pile of hay, stood a donkey.

"Have you been in here before?" said Abu Feisal, going across to the donkey and laying a work-calloused hand on its stiff, wiry mane.

"Yes, I suppose so," said Karim.

"I was born in this room," said Abu Feisal. "This is where your grandparents lived, and your greats, and their greats, for hundreds of years, in this one and the other room next to it. Your grandfather, God rest him, built the modern house in front, with the money he earned in Saudi Arabia. But this is the old family home."

Karim looked round. He couldn't imagine how the room must once have been, how people had really lived in here.

"They slept here and everything?"

Abu Feisal was gathering up the scattered hay into a pile and pushing it under the donkey's nose.

"Yes. It was cool in the summer and warm in winter. Not bad at all. Not modern, of course. We had oil lamps for lights and no running water. Just like it'll be in the future if the settlers go on shooting our water tanks and taking all our water."

He ran a hand down the donkey's back. The grey flank twitched and the sleepy animal lifted a hoof and flicked its tail.

"He had a sore on his back, here," said Abu Feisal. "It's healed up now. I'm still keeping an eye on it, though."

Karim went up to the donkey and looked. He could hardly see where the sore had been. The sweet smell of its breath and the calm way it stood were soothing.

Abu Feisal sat down on a full sack of animal feed and looked up at Karim from under his heavy white eyebrows.

"You've had a bad day," he observed.

Karim felt as if the blood was rushing to his head.

"Nobody does anything!" he burst out. "My father—they stripped him! Then they shot at him—us—in our own olive groves! But he doesn't do anything. And back in there, when they all heard about the bomber—the martyr—all they could talk

62

about was whether they'd get home all right or not. I feel so—so ashamed!"

He slumped down onto a sack opposite his uncle.

For a moment, Abu Feisal said nothing. Then he reached down for a wisp of straw and began twirling it between his fingers.

"It's not simple," he said at last. "Nothing's simple."

"It is, *sidi*, it is! They take our land and kill us. We should fight back and kill them. That's justice! That's all there is!"

Abu Feisal tucked his robe around his feet.

"Listen. I'll tell you something. When they first occupied us, in 1967, long before you were born, I was here in the village, working on the farm. I was young, like you, but I had time, every day, to think things over. There's always time for thinking, on the farm. I said to myself, 'Maybe they're right. Maybe they are better than us, and they have the right to take our land and do what they want with it. Maybe we really are the worthless, ignorant people they say we are.'"

Karim's face was red with anger and he was wriggling impatiently on the sack. His uncle took no notice.

"So I watched them closely, for a long time. I was trying to decide if they were superior beings or not. In the end, I saw that they were not. They were bad, good, moral, immoral, some greedy and vain, some kind-hearted and suffering, all just men, women, and children—like the rest of us. Human beings."

"Human? You call those settlers human?"

"Yes. Human. Like us. And that's what I find so depressing. Watching them, I see what we humans are capable of. I know that we could be like them too. They've shown me how bad human nature can be. If we had power over them, or over anyone else, for that matter, we'd do the same things that they do. It's what happens when the conquerors rule the conquered. The powerful hate their victims or they wouldn't be able to bear the thought of what they're doing to them. In their eyes we're nothing—inferior, barely human. They can't abide the knowledge that I learned long ago—that we're all the same."

Karim was silent for a moment, then, half under his breath, he said, *"We're* not bad. They are. Look at how many Palestinian kids they've murdered. We throw stones at them. They shoot bullets at us, to kill."

"So, does it make it right for us to go and bomb them? Those schoolkids who died today—they were probably the same age as you or Jamal. Did they deserve to die? How do you think their families feel tonight? And what about the ones who were injured? Legs and arms blown off, scarred for life, blind maybe?"

Karim could hardly bear to listen to his uncle any longer.

"They hate us. They're trying to destroy us. I hate them, all of them. I don't care how old they are. It's simple, *sidi*, like I said. As simple as that."

Abu Feisal laughed, but his eyes were sad.

"You think that now, but you'll remember what I said. It's not really that simple at all."

Everyone, except for the children, was still sitting at the table when Karim and his uncle went back into the room. No one seemed to have noticed that they'd been gone.

A sort of desperate cheerfulness was in the air.

"Have another olive," Um Hassan was saying, as she pushed the earthenware bowl of gleaming green olives across the table to her daughter-in-law. "Who knows whether we'll have any at all to pick next year?"

Lamia leaned back from the table and patted her stomach.

"I couldn't. I've eaten so much already."

"Well, why should we worry?" said a cousin, drawing the bowl towards himself and picking out an olive. "The Israelis love us so much they'll pick our olives for us next year and sell them to us at a special price—a high one."

The joke raised a few smiles, but nobody laughed.

"*Wallah*," sighed an old aunt. "When will these people go away and leave us alone?"

"When did anyone leave us alone?" said Abu Feisal, who had taken his place near the foot of the table. "Before the Israelis snatched our land it was the British who were our colonial masters. Three men they killed from this very village. And in my grandfather's day it was the Turks."

"One day, one day, *inshallah*," began the old aunt.

"We should be like the bombers and kill as many as we can," interrupted Karim, looking defiantly at his uncle.

"I'm not a fool. It's emigration for me," said a cousin.

Hassan Aboudi had sat in silence throughout the meal, but now he straightened his back and looked around the table.

"Endurance," he said. "That's what takes courage. Decency among ourselves. That's where we must be strong. When they steal from us and try to humiliate us, the real shame is on themselves."

Karim looked at him. His father had seemed shrunken, somehow, before the meal had started, but now he was himself again, a whole man. Karim felt a rush of love for him that took him by surprise. He wanted to run around the table and put his arms around his father's neck. The idea of making such an exhibition of himself was so embarrassing that he felt a blush spread over his face.

"The shame is on themselves," Hassan Aboudi repeated gravely.

Suddenly, Karim felt immensely tired. An unstoppable yawn gathered in his chest, puffed out his lungs and forced his mouth wide open. Lamia noticed.

"We should go to bed early," she said. "We ought to be on the road by seven thirty. There's no knowing how long the journey home will take."

Chapter Nine

It was good to be back in Ramallah, in spite of the almost tangible air of dread and expectancy that haunted the town in the wake of the suicide bombing. Hassan Aboudi pulled up in the parking space outside the flats and the little girls tumbled out at once. Farah was halfway up the first flight of stairs before Karim had even disengaged the headset of his Walkman from his ears and opened the door on his side of the car. "Rasha!" Farah was calling out. "I'm home! Rasha!"

Karim was about to follow her into the building when his mother called out, "Where are you going, Karim? Come and help me unload the trunk. I can't possibly manage all this myself."

Irritated, Karim took from her hands the basket stuffed with drooping vegetables that she was holding out to him.

It was up to him as usual to do the chores. Farah always seemed to get off with doing nothing, though he could remember clearly, when he was eight, he'd had to help his mother all the time.

At least the journey home hadn't been too bad. He'd been as tense as a coiled spring as they'd neared the checkpoint, only to find that it had gone. A mess of barbed wire and a couple of heavy boulders, which the tank had pushed across the road, half blocking it, were all that remained. The traffic, much too heavy anyway for such a small lane, was having to slow to a crawl to get past. Karim had shut his eyes as they came to the place where his father had been so humiliated. The spot was already etched indelibly on his memory. He didn't want to look at it again.

There'd been two more checkpoints to get through further on, and at the second one they'd been kept waiting for twenty minutes, for no apparent reason, but they'd been waved through at last, keeping their faces carefully immobile under the gaze of the soldiers and muttering their curses only under their breath.

The bags that Lamia had given him to carry seemed to weigh a ton. It was always like this when they came home from the village. Grandma and the aunts loaded them down with produce from their vegetable plots, fruit trees and storerooms—bags of onions and lemons, bundles of spinach, swags of fresh mint and parsley, and bottles of pickles, olives and oil.

"Take them while you can," Grandma had said to Lamia, pressing yet another bunch of homegrown grapes on her daughter-in-law. "Who knows how long we'll be able to grow anything here at all? They've taken our olive terraces this year. Next year they might help themselves to our whole farm."

It was clear, when at last they got inside, that Jamal hadn't expected his family to return so soon. He was out, and there was no sign that serious study had been taking place. Dirty dishes were piled in the sink in the kitchen, and empty mugs and a drift of crumbs graced the coffee table between the sofa and the TV.

"You shouldn't have let him stay," Lamia grumbled to her husband, after she'd clicked her tongue disapprovingly at the mess. "If he's done half an hour's work in total I'd be amazed."

Hassan Aboudi rounded on her.

"You're sorry he wasn't with me at the checkpoint that day? You wish he'd come out with us to pick the olives? What a prime target for them he would have been! A seventeen-year-old boy!"

Lamia bit her bottom lip and edged past him into the kitchen.

Hassan Aboudi had switched on the TV.

Tanks entered Bethlehem this morning and a strict curfew has been imposed. In Ramallah, clashes between Palestinian youths and Israeli troops....

Karim blocked the voice out.

Home again, he thought sourly, feeling the familiar crackle of tension in the air.

He'd only been back for five minutes, but he felt the need to get out again at once. He fetched his ball from behind its usual chair, then sidled around the edge of the sofa, making for the door.

"I'm going to see Joni," he informed his father's hunched back.

Hassan Aboudi, who was fiddling with the remote control for the TV, grunted but didn't turn around to answer.

It was great to be outside and on his own. Karim stuck the ball firmly under his arm, walked across the parking lot and down the short road that led to the main street running up the hill. He had set off fast, anxious to get away from the apartments before anyone could call him back, but without realizing it his steps were getting shorter and slower.

Would he turn right when he reached the road and go to Joni's? Or would he skip off the other way, towards the refugee camp and Hopper?

Preoccupied with his thoughts, he almost bumped into Jamal, who was turning onto the street with a gift-wrapped package in his hand.

"Karim! What are you doing here?"

"We came home early. We just got back."

Jamal's eyes were widening with horror.

"All of you? Mama and Baba? They're back too?"

"You think I walked all the way from the village on my own? Of course they're back."

"But why? You were supposed to be staying till Thursday."

Images of his father at the side of the road and the settlers running towards him through the olive trees flashed through Karim's mind. He didn't know where to start.

"It was...they.... " he began.

Jamal wasn't listening anyway.

"When did you arrive?"

"Just now. I told you."

"Has Mama been into our room yet?"

"Not as far as I know. I have, though."

Karim pursed his lips.

"No need to look like that, Mr. Clever-clever. I was going to get down to work this afternoon. I thought I had loads of time."

Karim's eyes narrowed suspiciously.

"What've you been doing, then? Did you go down to the tanks? There was something about clashes in Ramallah on the news."

Jamal shook his head, and the wedge of dark hair flopped against his forehead.

"No. None of my friends went out. Everyone's jumpy because of the military operation."

"The bomb?"

"Yes."

They looked at each other in silence. Karim tapped the package that Jamal was holding.

"What's this?"

Red began to flush through Jamal's cheeks. He jerked the parcel away.

"Lay off, Karim. Mind your own business."

Jamal seemed about to push past his brother and hurry on, but then he stopped and grabbed him by an elbow, almost dislodging the ball.

"Have you done anything about that photo yet?"

Karim shook him off.

"Are you crazy? I've been in the village, remember? Or do you think that there are photos of Violette scattered around down there?

Lying around the lanes, maybe? Stuck up on the trees? Anyway, speaking of trees, you wouldn't believe what happened. Our olives, the ones on the far side of the village, well, the settlers—"

But Jamal had started walking away.

"Yeah, well, tell me later. And don't forget the photo. You promised."

He was running now towards the entrance of the apartment building. He'd be up the stairs in a flash, Karim knew, and into the bedroom. He'd have the computer games swept away and his books laid out, with a bit of luck, before Mama had stuck her head through the doorway.

Karim put Jamal out of his mind. He'd reached the road now. He turned right. He'd go and see Joni. This business of the photograph—he'd better get it over and done with or Jamal would never give him any peace. He was regretting his promise already. What kind of fool would he look like, begging Joni for a photo of his stupid sister? Joni would be sure to think he wanted it for himself. He could already see the look on his friend's face, scornful and disbelieving. Contemptuous.

He slowed down again. He wasn't ready to see Joni yet. He needed to think up some kind of reason for getting the photo first. A story of some kind.

Anyway, there's no point in trying to see him, he thought. The Israelis didn't touch his school. He'll be there now.

He spun around and started off in the opposite direction, towards the refugee camp, his spirits lifting. This was what he'd wanted to do all along. He'd go back to the new soccer place and see if Hopper was there. Even if he wasn't, he could clear a few more stones and try playing his game against the wall. It might not be any good, against such an irregular surface, what with the holes in it and everything, but the challenge might make it even better. Anyway, it would be fun to give it a try.

Hopper's soccer place was nearer than he remembered. He'd been walking fast, but he stopped when he came level with the house where Hopper had said he lived.

I could go in there and ask for him, he told himself doubtfully. But he knew he wouldn't.

After all, I don't even know his real name.

A woman came around the side of the house from the back. She was wearing the long traditional Palestinian dress and a white headscarf. She was leaning over to one side, bowed down under the weight of the sack she was carrying.

She caught sight of Karim standing and staring at her from over the wall at the end of the vegetable plot, and shaded her eyes to see better.

"You want something?" she shouted across at him. Her voice was loud and cracked, with the accent of the coast. "What are you staring at? Never seen a sack of flour before?"

Taken by surprise, not knowing what to say, Karim turned and bounded away, hot with embarrassment. Her raucous laughter followed him down the hill.

As he'd expected, no one was at the empty plot. He walked across it towards the wall at the far end. It felt different being here without Hopper, almost as if he was trespassing. He pushed the feeling aside, put the ball down and gave it a tentative kick. It hit a projecting stone and glanced off sideways, as he'd guessed it would.

He retrieved it and kicked again, aiming more carefully this time, towards a smoother stone. The ball came back to him at a perfect angle. Pleased, he tried again. This wall was going to demand far more concentration than the one back at his flats. It could be really good. It would make him work harder, shoot more accurately, hone his skills.

He moved back to take a longer shot, and realized only after the ball had bounced sharply to one side and he'd had to fetch it, that there were fewer stones lying around on the ground than there had been before. The cleared area was bigger. Someone had been here. They must have worked hard to shift so much rubble.

Hopper, I bet it's him, Karim thought, grinning with pleasure at the idea.

He decided to work on it himself. He parked his ball between two stones, where it couldn't roll away, and looked around. He'd start over there, by the scraggly thorn bush. He'd see if he could clear the whole expanse between the wall and a rusting abandoned fridge before he went home.

Hopper appeared as suddenly and silently as he had the first time they'd met, materializing out of thin air just as Karim picked up the last broken cinder block and hurled it away onto the growing pile of stones.

"I didn't think I'd see you again," Hopper said curtly. "Thought you'd gone off for good in that car of yours."

He was the same boy, taut, tall and skinny as before, but the friendly smile had gone from his face.

Karim suddenly remembered the last time they'd met, when Hopper had leaned so confidently into the car and been so coldly greeted. He bit his lip, ashamed.

"We only went to our village. We got home this morning. I came here right away."

"Where's your village, then?"

"It's called Deir Aldalab. My grandma still lives there, and loads of cousins. It's only about half an hour away by car usually, but it took us hours. They stopped us for ages at the roadblocks."

"Lucky you to have a village," Hopper said lightly, spinning around to kick a broken plastic oil can away to the side. "My grandma's village is a suburb of Tel Aviv now. She hasn't seen it since the Israelis chased her family out of it in 1948."

Karim didn't know what to say, but Hopper didn't seem to expect an answer. He was looking around the area that Karim had cleared.

"Did you see how much I did yesterday?" he said.

"Yes. It's great. Must have taken you ages."

They grinned at each other, all constraint gone.

"You brought your ball, then," said Hopper, nodding over to where the ball still lay, held between the stones.

Karim picked it up and without saying anything more kicked it against the wall. It hit the perfect spot, precisely where he'd aimed it, and bounced back smoothly towards Hopper. Hopper shot out one stringy leg and took an ungainly swipe at it. The ball hit a jagged stone and careered up into the air. Hopper grunted, displeased with himself, as Karim ran forward to catch it on his knee.

They played on in silence, taking it in turns to kick. Karim was the most skillful. When he had time to position himself, his aim was seldom off, but Hopper tended to shoot the ball back fast and wild, sending it glancing unpredictably in every direction. It made the game exciting. A lot more fun.

"That was great," panted Karim, when they'd stopped at last and had sunk down, red-faced and sweating, onto the pile of stones they'd made.

"I'm thirsty," said Hopper. "Let's go to my house and get a drink."

Karim remembered the woman with the sack of flour and felt shy.

"No, I've got to go home. I'll get in trouble if I'm late." He caught the look of faint contempt in Hopper's eyes and turned away, wishing he'd said yes. "I'll come tomorrow if I can. If school hasn't started yet."

"It won't have. Didn't you see the mess the Israelis made? They've wrecked everything. Taken the computers, smashed up the desks and stuff. It'll be another week at least before we can go back."

"All right then." Karim turned to go. "I'll come back tomorrow. At the same time."

"OK. See you."

"Yes. See you."

Karim scooped up the ball with his foot and flicked it with a deft upward kick into his hands. He looked at his watch. It was later than he'd thought. He crossed the soccer field at a trot and set off up the hill.

As he neared the top, he heard running steps behind him and turned. Hopper was streaking up after him.

"I'll come with you as far as the school," he said, falling into a long, easy stride beside him. "Just to see how it's going."

Karim shrugged.

"OK."

The soccer field at school was almost unrecognizable now. The goalposts and nets lay broken on the ground, and the surface, normally a smooth flatness of bare earth, had been churned up into mounds and ridges by the tracks of the tanks that had been assembled there. Broken desks and chairs, cleared out of the vandalized classrooms, lay in a pile outside the main entrance. Workmen were climbing ladders up the sides of the building, carrying blocks and cement to patch the walls where tank shells had left several jagged holes. Still more were picking shards of broken glass out of the window frames.

"See what I mean?" said Hopper. "It'll be ages before we go back."

"Karim!" someone called out.

Karim turned. Joni was hurrying down the hill towards him.

Karim felt awkward. What would Hopper think of Joni, in his smart private-school uniform? And what would Joni make of Hopper, a scruffy boy from the refugee camp?

"I've got to go," he mumbled to Hopper, and, without looking back, he walked up to meet Joni.

Joni executed a couple of karate kicks, nearly lost his balance and grabbed Karim's arm for support.

"Didn't know you were back yet," he said. "I'm going into town. Want to come with me?"

He was moving off already, down the hill past the school.

"OK, but let's go this way," said Karim, turning away from Hopper.

"Why? That way's much further."

"No, it isn't."

"You know it is. We always go this way. What's the matter with you?"

Karim shrugged, irritated.

"Nothing. I don't feel like town anyway. And I've got to go home. I'm expected. Come with me."

"No. Mama wants me to get some stuff from the pharmacy. What are you doing around here anyway? Who's that boy?"

"No one. I've been playing soccer, that's all."

Joni glanced down towards the school's wrecked playground.

"Soccer? Where? Not down there."

Karim opened his mouth, then shut it again. This was stupid. Everything was getting tangled up. He didn't know how to straighten things out.

Joni was looking insulted.

"Don't tell me, then. I don't care anyway."

He tried to pass Karim. Karim dodged in front of him.

"Why have you got to go to the pharmacy?" he asked, trying to hold Joni back till he could put things right.

Joni wasn't mollified.

"Violette's ill. She's got the flu. She needs some stuff."

This would have been the moment. This was the time to slap Joni on the shoulder, be all breezy and casual, man to man, and say something cool and amusing, like, "Speaking of Violette, you'll never guess what. My stupid brother has a crush on your crazy sister and he wants you to give him a photo of her."

But there was no chance of that now. Joni was annoyed. He'd

moved past Karim and was away down the hill, the very lines of his back looking offended. He passed Hopper without a sideways glance.

Karim kicked at a broken piece of pavement so hard that he thought for an agonizing moment that he'd splintered his toe. He squeezed his eyes tight shut with the pain, then opened them as it receded and shot a resentful look at Hopper, who was still leaning casually against the school wall, looking up at him.

Turning his back on him, Karim limped off for home, cursing under his breath.

Chapter Ten

Automatically, without noticing what he was doing, Karim took the long way home, dragging his sore foot for a few minutes, until the pain wore off, heading down the road that led past the smart new villas of the government men. Israeli tanks had trashed this part of town. The tall metal streetlights, installed only recently, were bent into strange shapes, some toppling right over. They looked like vast, wounded insects. Parts of the pavement were smashed up. In other places, regular diamond-shaped chips had been sliced from the curbstones by the tanks' tracks.

Karim hardly noticed the destruction. His head was full of his own stupidity.

What does it matter, he thought, if Joni meets Hopper? What am I making such a fuss about?

He could see Joni in his mind's eye, as clearly as if he was standing right in front of him. They'd been best friends for so long he never bothered, usually, to think about him at all. Joni, with his round face, his plumpness, his perfectly ironed clothes, his not-very-good karate kicks, his jokey talk and clever ideas—Joni was as familiar to him as the red furry blanket on his bed, closer than Jamal, more necessary even than his parents.

How could he possibly have quarrelled with Joni?

But it was Hopper he could see now, the boy from nowhere, the sharp one, the unpredictable, secret, forbidden friend. He wanted to be friends with Hopper too.

He tried to imagine the two boys together, side by side. He couldn't. They were as different from each other as an eagle from a rooster, or—or a cactus from a sunflower.

Hopper would think Joni was soft, he thought. Joni would think Hopper was rough.

He was still lost in thought when he arrived home.

"Karim!" He came to with a start as he registered the sharpness in his mother's voice. "Where on earth have you been?"

He was surprised by her intensity.

"Out."

"Where? Who with? What have you been doing?"

"Playing soccer," he said truthfully, holding the ball out as proof.

She pushed up the sleeves of her heavy brown sweater, crossed her arms and stared at him suspiciously.

"Where? Not in the usual place. I went down to look for you. How can you do this to me, Karim? You know how worried I get."

He was beginning to feel cornered.

"I met a guy from school. We played near his place."

"Oh."

She hesitated, and seemed about to say more, when a crash from the kitchen followed by a wail from Sireen sent her hurrying off to investigate.

Karim parked his ball behind its usual chair and went to his bedroom. Jamal was sitting on the edge of his bed, strumming inexpertly on the battered guitar he'd acquired in a swapping deal with a friend. He was crooning tunelessly:

Don' break my heart, baby,
Don' tear my mind apart.

He looked up, saw the astonished disgust on Karim's face and hastily put the guitar down.

"What's got into Mama?" Karim said, flopping onto his own bed. "What's she yelling at me for?"

Jamal grinned.

"She thought you were a) dead, b) carted off to an Israeli prison, c) blowing yourself up in martyrdom, d) unconscious in the hospital with a broken skull, e) dead."

He was ticking the points off on his fingers.

"You said 'dead' twice," Karim pointed out.

"That's because she said it twice. That she thought you were dead, I mean. More than twice. About 150 times, actually."

"But I've only been out a couple of hours. Three at the most."

"Join the club." Jamal stood up and stretched. "Be warned. You are now entering the peak maternal worry zone. I've been inhabiting it for years, or haven't you noticed? It's the price you pay for the approach of manhood. Our dear mother, from now on, will pester you endlessly every time you go out and come home again, and Baba probably will too."

Karim was torn between pleasure that Jamal realized he was approaching manhood and irritation at the prospect of increased parental interference.

"What a pain," he said, trying for a sophisticated lightness of touch.

"It is, my son, it is. But there are dodges. Ways and means. A little ingenuity is all that is required. You'll learn."

The patronage in his tone irritated Karim. He looked around for something cutting to remark on, and saw the gift-wrapped package lying on Jamal's pillow.

"Thanks for the present," he said, reaching over to snatch it up.

Jamal's hand closed as quick as a whiplash on his wrist.

"Don't you dare touch that, you little animal!"

"Ooh," said Karim, shaking him off. "Temper, temper. What is it, then? *Violet*-scented soap? A *purple* scarf? A picture of *flowers*?"

Jamal cuffed him back down onto his bed.

"Mind your own business, baby boy."

"It is my business. I'm supposed to be getting ahold of her photo, remember?"

"Mm." Jamal looked uncertain. "Well, if you must know, it's a necklace. And I know she likes it because I overheard her friends discussing it when they were looking into the window of Fancy Stores. I'm going to give it to her tomorrow. She and her gang are all going to the movies. So keep your dirty little hands off it till then, if you please."

"You can save yourself some trouble," said Karim, enjoying his moment of superiority. "Her friends may be going to the cinema, but Violette won't be, as I know to my certain knowledge."

"What? Why not?"

"She's got the flu. Her eyes are all red and her nose is running and she's coughing up disgusting gobs of—"

His sentence finished in a squeal as Jamal sat on him. He managed, after a violent struggle, to shake him off and sit up.

"How come you can afford to go around buying necklaces, anyway?" he panted. "We haven't had any pocket money for months. Not since the uprising began."

"I told you," said Jamal, not meeting his eyes. "Dodges. Ways and means."

"What ways and means? You didn't—you couldn't have stolen it!"

Jamal frowned.

"Do you mind? I'm not a thief. I sold something to a friend, if you must know. Got a good price for it, actually."

"What did you sell? What was it?"

"Only an old computer game. We've played it so often it's gotten really boring. We don't want it any more."

A chill was running down Karim's back.

"What computer game? Which one?"

Jamal backed away, took hold of a chair and put it between himself and Karim.

"Lineman. But look, it's just an old—it's boring, you know it is. It's out of date. It's—Karim! Stop it! Watch what you're doing. Karim!"

It was a miracle, Karim thought sourly twenty minutes later, that the noise of their fight hadn't brought their mother in to intervene. He wouldn't have minded for once. He'd have been quite prepared to tell her the whole story, the whole stupid business about Violette, and watch Jamal go purple with embarrassment, and squirm like a worm on a hook. But Mama hadn't come in. Rasha's mother had appeared at the front door, and the two women had been outside in the hallway, absorbed in their conversation.

Jamal seemed taken aback by the ferocity of Karim's anger.

"You had no *right!*" Karim spat at him again and again. "Lineman's mine just as much as yours. I hate you. I *hate* you!"

"Yes, OK. Yes, well, I'm sorry," Jamal kept saying. "Look, I'll make it up to you. Just lay off, will you?"

"Make it up to me? How? I want Lineman back. I want it *back!*"

Eventually, they'd hammered out a compromise. Jamal would find something else to sell, maybe even his guitar, and he'd buy Lineman back, but only when the photograph of Violette was put into his hands. Once the deal had been done, judging no doubt wisely, that Karim would be better left alone, Jamal hooked his finger into the loop inside the collar of his leather jacket and, affecting a casual whistle, sauntered out of the apartment.

Sore and bruised, Karim brooded on his bed.

Life's so unfair, he thought. Everything's so unfair.

He could feel a heaviness descending on him, a lowering depression. He'd half forgotten, in the turbulence of the last few hours, the events in the village, the humiliation of his father and the unpunished thefts of the settlers, but they were sharply present in his mind again, pressing down on him. The loss of Lineman made everything seem suddenly far worse. It had been a refuge for him when the curfew was down, a release when things got too bad, a place he could go to in his mind when his body was held captive. Jamal had snatched it away in a callous act of betrayal.

I've got to get ahold of that stupid photograph, he told himself savagely. I've just got to get it. I'll call Joni now. I'll make everything right with him, and go round to his place, and sort it out straight away.

He reached out for the cell phone lying on the table. His own was useless. The card had run out weeks ago and he had no money to buy another. Jamal's was still working, though. He took a deep breath and punched in the familiar number. He could see in his mind's eye the apartment at the other end of the line where the phone must now be ringing. Rose, Joni's mother, would be in the kitchen. She'd hear it, run her hands under the tap, dry them off and reach out for it. Or perhaps Joni would hear it above the noise of the stereo that he kept on at full blast in his room. On balance, Karim hoped that Rose would get there first.

She did.

"Hello," Karim said, his voice sounding squeaky even to him. "It's Karim. Is—can I speak to Joni please?"

He heard Rose put the phone down at the other end and a sudden blast of sound as she opened Joni's bedroom door. He could practically see her plump, comfortable figure, her crown of permed hair and the fussy blouse she habitually wore. Muffled voices came next, then the slap of her slippers on the stone floor as she returned to the phone.

"He's—er—he's busy just now, Karim." He could hear the surprise in her voice. "Maybe he'll call you later, OK?"

"Thanks," muttered Karim, putting the phone back down. His heart had sunk even lower. Joni must be really annoyed. Genuinely hurt. It would take more than a simple phone call to bring him around.

Then something inside Karim rose up in revolt. What was Joni making such a big deal about anyway? He'd only been playing soccer with Hopper, for goodness' sake. Joni didn't own him. There was room in everyone's life for more than one friend.

Forget Joni. Forget everyone, Karim thought angrily. I'll go back to Hopper's field tomorrow, and the day after, and as often as I like. I don't care what anyone says.

Chapter Eleven

Reprisals for the suicide bomb were in full swing in Bethlehem, where the whole city had been shut down. Everyone was imprisoned in their homes by the Israeli army, and eight people had been killed by tank shells, while three houses had been demolished by enemy bulldozers, the inhabitants barely escaping with their lives. In Ramallah, though, there was still a jumpy state of normality.

"The university's reopened," Lamia said at breakfast the next morning. "I'll have to go to work. Though heaven knows how long it will take, with the roadblocks they've set up all over the place. I'll see if Rasha's mother can take care of Sireen."

Karim smiled secretly at the news. With his mother out of the way, Farah back at her primary school and Baba down at the shop, he'd be free to do what he pleased.

"Karim," Lamia began, turning towards him. She seemed about to issue an instruction of some kind, and Karim held his breath, fearing that his day of freedom was about to be snatched away, but at that moment someone knocked on the outer door and she went to open it.

Karim slipped off to his room. He'd wait till the neighbor had gone and Mama had left for work. With luck, she'd be in such a hurry to leave that she'd forget whatever it was she'd wanted him to do.

The coast was clear at last. Karim waited until the clack of his mother's shoes had faded away to the bottom of the stairs, then he ran to the kitchen balcony and watched her walk up the hill towards the bus stop. As if on cue, the bus came. She got on and it rolled away. Karim darted back to the living room, retrieved his ball and let himself out of the apartment, bounding down the stairs with a heady sense of freedom.

He didn't slow down till he came to the top of the hill above the school, but when he reached it, and could look back at the school and the refugee camp beyond, he came to a stop.

The Israeli tanks had been on the move again. One had parked just above the school, its massive brown bulk looming above the street. Soldiers in battle gear, with helmets and body armor, rifles cradled in their arms, were blocking the street, stopping everyone from passing.

Karim tightened his fists in frustration and anger. Whatever you tried to do in this country, wherever you wanted to go, the enemy was always there to stop you. Even a simple game of soccer was impossible.

One of the soldiers looked up and saw Karim, fixing his eyes on him intently. Trying to look casual, Karim turned and walked away. There was no telling what any of them would do if they felt threatened or were irritated. Being only twelve years old was no protection. Kids younger than him were shot all the time. These guys' fingers seemed to hover permanently on their triggers.

He walked disconsolately back the way he'd come. He could try getting to Hopper's ground (as he now called the place to himself) by going the long way around, climbing right up the opposite hill then circling over to the far side, but that would bring him up against the edge of one of the Israeli settlements that ringed Ramallah. The settlers there had a reputation for unpredictability. They'd been known to take pot shots at random passers-by. If Hopper had been with him, he might have risked it, just to prove

that he wasn't afraid, but he didn't feel like being a target on his own.

Slowly, he walked home. Perhaps, at long last, he should try to do a bit of homework. It had to be tackled sooner or later, after all.

The morning passed surprisingly quickly. Some of the work was boring, of course. He hurried through the geography questions and the English exercises as quickly as he could. But the history was unexpectedly interesting.

He'd been sent a passage to read about the ancient Egyptians. It described several different theories about the methods they'd used to build their vast pyramids and temples, how they'd succeeded in shifting the massive blocks of stone, carrying them up to such astonishing heights. He fiddled around for a while with the books and erasers and pens on the table, trying to construct a miniature pyramid, then was afflicted by a series of gigantic yawns. It was boring, being on his own. He'd even be quite glad when school started up again.

By midday, he was desperate to go out. He fetched some bread from the box on the kitchen counter, opened the fridge and scooped up some hummus, then grabbed some olives and ate those too. He took a long drink of water from the pitcher, then he ran out of the apartment and down the stairs to the street.

He wouldn't try to get to Hopper's ground. He'd go into the middle of town instead. He'd check out the price of those little instant throw-away cameras. If they weren't too expensive he might, somehow, find the money to buy one. Then, perhaps, if he managed to make it up with Joni, he could go to his house and sneak a few photos of Violette himself. He'd never used a camera, but it looked super-easy. You just had to point it and press the button. He'd never promised Jamal a good photo. Just a photo.

Having an aim, even such a vague one, made him feel quite purposeful. He walked fast and jauntily even, swinging around each broken lamppost as he came to it and kicking out at each scrap of paper or plastic bag that fluttered on the pavement.

An empty soda can lying in the gutter caught his eye. He picked it up on the end of his toe and began to dribble it up the hill. Concentrating on it, he was oblivious to everything else until the sound of shouting and the electronic stutter of a loudspeaker, telling people to move away, caught his attention.

The noise was coming from the left, from the dip at the bottom of the steep hill. An on-ramp here joined the fast highway that was for the exclusive use of Israeli settlers and was constantly patrolled by armored vehicles to keep Palestinians away.

Three of these vehicles were now clustered behind a heavy concrete barricade. People were running up the hill, away from them.

Curious, Karim took a few steps down the hill to get a closer look.

"Go back!" a man shouted at him. "There's a bomb down there on the settlers' road!"

"Where? Where is it?" Karim called back.

"Under the bridge over the gulley."

"Who put it there?"

"How should I know?" the man was past him already, calling over his shoulder. "They found it just now."

Karim was backing away, his pulse quickening, infected by the urgency of the people around him, when he caught sight of a thin figure, a boy in a white T-shirt and dusty trousers, who was climbing up the scaffolding at the side of a ruined, derelict building below, only a short way from the bridge.

Karim's eyes narrowed as he tried to make him out. It looked like Hopper. It was Hopper! What on earth was he doing down there? Why wasn't he running away like everyone else?

Karim had turned to run himself, but then he stopped and looked back. He felt as if Hopper was daring him, challenging him to climb the scaffolding too. As if he was saying, "*I'm* brave enough to do this. What are you? A wimp?"

Trying to ignore the prickling of his skin and the knot in his stomach, Karim began to walk down the hill against the flow of people.

"Are you crazy? They'll shoot you!" an old woman shouted at him.

"Don't go down there!" other people called out.

Hopper had reached the top of the scaffolding and had jumped down behind the low wall that ringed the roof of the building. He was out of sight.

Trying to make himself as invisible as possible, Karim edged down the road towards the bridge, keeping close to the side. If he could only reach the next opening in the long wall beside him, he could slip around behind it and work his way towards the scaffolding out of the sight of the soldiers. It would mean climbing over the ruins of a row of buildings that had been shelled to dereliction by Israeli tanks when the settlers' road had been built, but that wouldn't be impossible.

His scalp tingled with fright when he thought about what he was doing. Twice he stopped and almost turned back, and twice he went on again.

I'll just get a bit closer, he told himself. No need to decide yet if I'm actually going to go up there.

The crowd of people streaming up the hill had thinned out now. There was only one old woman, struggling to walk fast on rickety legs, and a young man bowed under the weight of a computer that he was carrying on his shoulders.

Karim had almost reached the gap in the wall, and was about to dart through it, when he heard footsteps running down behind him. He whipped around, and to his astonishment saw Joni.

"What are you doing, Karim?" Joni burst out, as soon as he was within earshot. "Are you crazy or what?"

Karim grabbed hold of Joni's arm and dragged him through the gap in the wall. Out of sight now, both from the people above and the Israelis below, they stood staring at each other.

"What are you doing here?" said Karim.

"I was going home. I came around this way to see my cousin. Then I heard all this fuss and saw you."

They stood and stared at each other.

"Are you trying to get killed or what?" Joni demanded. "Because I'm not going to let you."

Karim stared at his old friend. Joni was blinking rapidly and beads of sweat had sprouted on his round face. He was gripping his schoolbag so tightly that his knuckles showed white. He looked a little absurd, but oddly heroic too.

Affection washed over Karim.

"No, you moron. Of course I'm not trying to get killed. There's someone I know who's climbed up there onto the roof. I saw him go up the scaffolding. His name's Hopper. It's short for Grasshopper. He goes to my school."

"So? Hundreds of people go to your school."

"He's sort of different. He's from the refugee camp. He's the person I was playing soccer with the other day."

"When you wouldn't tell me where you'd been?"

"Yes. I don't know why I did that. I felt like a total fool afterwards. I thought you wouldn't like him or something. I was embarrassed. I thought you'd think he was weird. He is weird, but he's interesting too. Like I said—different."

A grin spread over Joni's face.

"You're the weird one. I thought you were totally mad at me or something."

"Yes, I know. I was an idiot. Sorry."

Sirens wailing through the air took their attention away from each other. Karim peered out cautiously through the gap in the wall.

"More soldiers," he said, "and one of their own ambulances. Must be a big bomb." He felt a surge of excitement and a longing for revenge. "I hope it goes off and totally wrecks their horrible road and blows them all up in their cars."

"It wasn't your friend, Hopper, or whatever you call him, who planted it, was it?" said Joni.

"Couldn't have been. Where would he get all the stuff from, the explosives and everything?"

"Then what's he doing up there on the roof?"

"That's what I wanted to find out. I thought I could work my way over the rubble without them seeing me and climb up after him."

Joni was blinking harder than ever.

He's really scared, thought Karim, but he's not going to admit it. Joni's fear made him feel braver.

"Look," he said. "You stay here and keep a lookout. I'll go ahead, and if you see anything funny—"

"I'm not going to let you go by yourself," Joni said, his voice tight. "I'm going with you."

For a long moment, neither of them spoke, and in the silence Karim felt something shift. Up till now, they'd been mere children, watching the struggle from the sidelines, keeping out of trouble as their parents had always urged them to do.

The approach of manhood, Jamal had said.

"Come on, then," he said. "Better leave your bag here. It'll get in the way."

Joni began to put it down, then shook his head.

"No. It's got my name on everything inside it. If they do a search and find it, they'll think I'm the bomber, and they'll trace me and demolish our house."

The piles of rubble seemed much bigger as they approached them, and the noise of the stones shifting under their feet was deafening against the silence which had fallen over the whole area. At last, though, they stood underneath the network of scaffolding which stretched up four floors above them to the top of the derelict building. It looked higher and yet less substantial close up.

Karim suddenly felt almost resentful. If Joni hadn't turned up, he'd probably have had the sense to give up and slip off home. There was no way back now, though, if he didn't want to lose respect.

"I'll go up first," Joni whispered, his face pale and set.

"No. Hopper doesn't know you. He might panic if he sees your ugly face suddenly pop up."

It was easier, in fact, to climb the scaffolding than Karim had imagined. He found he could swing up it quite quickly, though the distance from the ground, once he was past the second floor, seemed much further than he had expected.

How are we going to get back down again? he thought.

The very idea of it made him feel weak, and his palms began to sweat, but worse than the height was the feeling of exposure. He and Joni must be visible for miles around. If an Israeli soldier was to move just a short distance up the hill, he'd spot them at once. He'd probably assume they were the bombers and simply blow them away.

The idea terrified him so much that he put on a violent spurt, forgetting his fear of falling, and a few minutes later had reached the wall edging the roof and had jumped over it onto the flat surface of the roof itself.

He was just in time. An engine was starting up below. It was moving up the hill. At any moment, the scaffolding would be in full view of the Israelis, and Joni would stand out against it as obvious and helpless as a butterfly pinned to a card.

He leaned over the side of the building.

"Joni! Quick! They're coming!" he hissed.

Joni looked up at him, his face a white mask of fright.

"I can't move! My shirt's caught!"

Karim could see where the shirt had snagged on one of the scaffold bolts. Joni's frantic efforts to work it free, impeded by his bag, were only pulling it tighter.

The vehicle seemed to be moving slowly, thank God, but it was still coming. It would appear at any moment.

"Don't panic, I'm coming down," Karim called softly. He gritted his teeth, trying to summon up the courage to move, but before he could get a leg over the wall, someone else came up beside him and shot over the edge. It was Hopper.

In a flash, Hopper had swarmed down the scaffolding, released the caught shirt and practically hauled Joni and his bag up the last few feet. Together, they rolled over the wall and out of sight just as the armored vehicle came alongside the end of the building.

For a moment, the three of them lay motionless. Karim couldn't have moved or spoken if he'd tried. His heart was thudding so furiously that he was afraid it would break open.

Hopper was the first to recover. He sat up, frowning fiercely at the other two.

"What the hell are you doing here, Karim? And who's this?"

"He's Joni. He's my friend," Karim said. "What are you doing here anyway?"

"It's my bomb," Hopper said, as if surprised at being asked. "Did they see you? If they did, that's it. We're dead."

Karim was staring at him, open-mouthed.

"What do you mean, your bomb? How did you make it? Where did you get all the stuff from?"

Hopper had grabbed his arm and was shaking it.

"Did they see you? Did anyone see you?"

"I don't think so."

The three of them looked back cautiously over the edge of the scaffolding. A higher building a little further up the hill effectively blocked all sight of them from the town above, and as long as they kept below the wall, they were invisible to anyone on the ground below. Joni and Karim both let out sighs of relief. A reluctant grin was spreading across Hopper's face.

"Now you're here," he said, "you might as well see the fun."

He began to creep towards the far side of the roof. Several holes had been punched through the wall here in a previous bout of shelling. Cautiously, Hopper crawled towards one of these and looked out. The other two peered over his shoulder.

Below, they could clearly see the bridge, and, just underneath it, a bulging plastic bag, its whiteness startling in the brown shadows. It would have looked like nothing more than a piece of discarded garbage except for the little forest of wires, which, even from here, they could see protruding from it.

"That's it?" whispered Joni. "That's the bomb?"

"*You* made it?" said Karim. "*You* put it there?"

Hopper nodded. He was hugging himself with delight.

The Israeli vehicles were out of sight from here, protected behind the concrete embrasure on the far side of the bridge, and the only people visible were three men wearing transparent face shields and heavy body protectors.

"The bomb-disposal squad," murmured Hopper. "It'll take them ages."

From this vantage point, a long stretch of the settlers' road was visible. Traffic from the settlement was beginning to build up beyond the roadblock that the soldiers had hastily erected. Irritated drivers were leaning out of their windows, gesticulating to the soldiers and to each other.

"You can just wait for once. Let's see how you like it," Hopper crowed quietly.

"But the bomb," said Karim. "How did you—I mean, the explosives and everything. Weren't you scared of blowing yourself up?"

"Scared of a few stones, some paper, a load of old wires, and some sticky tape?" scoffed Hopper. "What do you take me for?"

"You mean it's not real? It's a hoax?" said Karim. He felt a mixture of relief and disappointment.

Beside him, Joni was trying to suppress an eruption of laughter.

"Hopper, you are—you're awesome!" he managed to say at last.

Hopper turned and looked at him. Karim couldn't read his expression. Did it show contempt or indifference? Hostility even?

"What did you say your name was?" Hopper said curtly.

"Joni. Joni Boutros."

"You're not related to Zuhair Hussein, are you?"

"Who?"

"Zuhair Hussein."

"How could I be? That's a Muslim name. I'm Christian."

"He goes to our school. He's a creep. You look like him, that's all."

"Oh? So there's another guy around who's as handsome as me, huh?"

Karim, watching the action below, was only half listening to his friends' prickly conversation. It seemed surreal to be up here, on this rooftop, in great danger, while the two of them circled round each other like a couple of sniffing dogs. He was surprised by Hopper's initial resentment, and amazed by Joni's coolness and charm. It seemed to be working on Hopper. Karim sensed that he had relaxed, and when he turned around to look he saw that Hopper was actually grinning.

"You're a couple of nut-jobs, coming up here," he said, including Karim in his smile. "You know what'll happen if they see us? They'll shoot straight off."

"Better keep out of sight, then," said Karim. He spoke lightly, although his stomach was churning.

He tugged at Joni's sleeve to pull him back into the shelter of the wall. Joni's shirt, washed to a luminous brightness by Rose, would be as visible as a flag to anyone below.

A soldier had crept right up to the plastic bag now and was peering at it cautiously. The backs of the other two were turned so that Karim couldn't see what they were doing.

"They'll be doing a controlled explosion," Joni said knowledgeably. "Blowing it up themselves."

The men seemed to have finished their preparations. They moved away from the bridge. One called out urgently in Hebrew, and then they were out of sight.

The explosion, although it was barely more than a dull thud, made the three boys jump. Dust was billowing up from below the bridge. For a few minutes they could make out nothing, but then, as the breeze blew the dust away, they saw the three soldiers emerge from the far side of the embankment. The bag had disappeared, but shreds of white plastic and torn paper were swirling around in the air, fluttering down slowly to the ground. One of the men kicked out in exasperation at the settling drift of debris. Another pulled him aside, bent down and picked something up. He showed it to the others, shouted something that sounded like a curse and hurled it away up the hillside on the far side of the settlers' road.

"What was that? Was it something you put in the bomb?" said Karim.

Hopper was grinning delightedly.

"It was a stone. I wrote 'Free Palestine' on one side, 'Death to Israel' on the other and 'Suckers' along the edges."

"Oh, wow! That is so cool!" Joni's mouth was hanging open in admiration.

"But they can't read Arabic," objected Karim.

"I wrote it in English."

He was about to say something else when all three of them became aware of a piercing, droning sound that was getting louder all the time.

"A helicopter!" gasped Karim. "They're searching the area. They're sure to see us! We're going to get caught!"

Hopper, wasting no time, was scanning the large open rooftop.

"Under the water tanks, over there," he said. "We've got to hide."

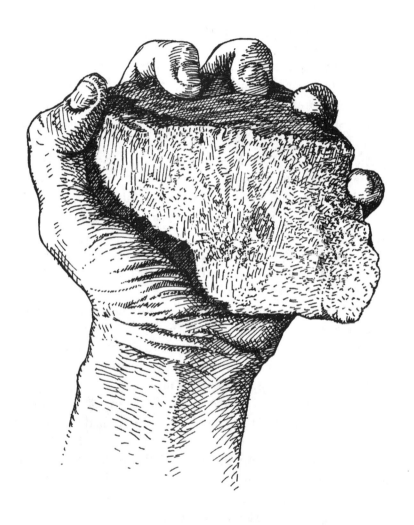

"That's no good." Karim's mind was racing. "They might have heat-seeking devices. They'll detect us. We've got to get down inside the building."

"Too late! Quick! It's coming!"

Hopper was already scampering over the bare concrete.

"There's room! Come on!" he called out.

The others squeezed in beside him. There wasn't much space under the platform on which the water tanks (long since holed by settler sniper fire) still stood, but the boys crushed in against each other, desperate to pull out of sight every arm, leg and shred of clothing.

The helicopter was overhead already. It was hovering now, filling the air with the deafening, whining beat of its propeller. It seemed so close that a hand reaching up could touch it.

It's seen us. It's going to land right here. They'll have machine guns. We're going to die, thought Karim.

His eyes were squeezed tightly shut. His hands closed onto the nearest thing to him and gripped it compulsively.

This is it! This is it! This is it!

The words pulsed in his head to the rhythm of the sweeping blades above.

The seconds passed infinitely slowly. Karim felt a wild urge to end it quickly, to crawl out from under the platform's shelter and jump up, screaming, "Go on! Do it! Kill us!"

Then, suddenly, it was over. The great shrieking machine wheeled away through the sky and seconds later had disappeared over the brow of the hill.

The boys burst out from under the platform with the energy of springs released from pressure. Karim felt sick. Even Hopper looked green. Astonishingly, Joni was the coolest of them all. He was bending down to examine his ankle.

"You maniac, Karim. Were you trying to wrench my foot off or what? You were squeezing it so tight you've probably cut off the blood supply and I'm going to die of gangrene."

Karim looked abashed.

"Sorry. I sort of needed something to hang on to."

"Yeah, the way Joni was crushing my arm," Hopper said, fingering his elbow. "Come on. Let's get the hell out of here."

They crawled back to the gap in the wall and peered out. The roadblock had been lifted and the settler traffic was on the move again. The ambulance had gone but the armored vehicles were still there. Several soldiers were clustered near them and one was talking into a mobile phone. They were all on the far side of the building now, and the scaffolding was out of their sight.

"We've got to be quick," Karim said. "They'll search the whole area."

It was horrible climbing down the scaffolding, scarier, even, than climbing up it had been, but when at last they stood on the solid ground again, relief sent waves of euphoria through them. Minutes later, they had scrambled back over the piles of rubble, run up to the top of the hill, and were standing in the relative safety of the street above, three boys indistinguishable from any others, dancing around with crows of delight as they looked down at the scene of their triumph.

Chapter Twelve

It seemed the most natural thing in the world, after all that had happened, to go to Hopper's ground. The three boys didn't even need to talk about it. Something unexpected had happened on the bare rooftop. They had become a trio.

"Too bad I haven't got my ball," Karim said when they arrived. "We could have had a real game."

He was watching Joni as he spoke, trying to work out his reaction to the place.

"What do you want to do here?" Joni asked. Karim couldn't tell if he was enthusiastic or not.

"Play soccer, what else?" he said defensively.

"Why? You got another idea?" said Hopper, propping his shoulders against the wall. He had pulled a dry grass stem out from between the stones and was rolling it between his teeth.

"Yes, well, it's got *possibilities*." Joni was walking around, picking up scraps of metal and old plastic buckets, looking over the walls, measuring distances with his eyes. "We could do things here. Make something of it."

"Yeah. We could play soccer." Karim was beginning to feel irritated.

Hopper was studying Joni. He took the straw out of his mouth. "Do what? Make what?"

"I dunno. I'm only thinking. Like—I mean, over there. Isn't that a wrecked car under all that rubble? We could clean it out.

Make a sort of base. Those oil drums. Maybe we could do something with them."

"I know what you want," Karim said impatiently. "A place to do karate in."

"You know karate?" Hopper peeled himself off the wall and leaned forward, looking interested.

Instead of answering, Joni took up a martial position, raised his hands and kicked. He lost his balance and almost fell over.

"He *thinks* he knows karate," Karim said. "Meet the number-one ace champion gold-medalist martial arts expert of the entire world. Of Palestine, anyway. Well, of Ramallah. OK, of this bit of it, maybe."

"All right, all right, funny man," said Joni, steadying himself.

Hopper had moved away from them and was examining the mountain of rubble.

"You're right, though, about the car. We could clear all this stuff away and get into it. That would be good. We'd have a place to go. A place of our own."

He bent down and pulled at a length of plastic pipe that was sticking out of the heap. A hearty tug brought a cascade of old cans, plastic bottles, broken tiles and ripped curtains tumbling down. The driver's side of the car, from which the doors had been ripped off, was now fully revealed.

"It's still got seats in it," said Karim. He was interested now. He could see this might be fun.

Hopper was working at the rubble with both hands, tearing it away to reveal more and more of the car. He drew back suddenly with an exclamation of pain and stuck his thumb into his mouth.

"What's the matter?" said Joni.

"Nothing. I cut myself. Broken glass."

Joni reached into his bag and pulled out a new tissue from a packet. He handed it to Hopper, who wrapped it around his thumb and raised his eyebrows towards Karim.

"I know," said Karim. "He carries packets of tissues."

He thumped Joni affectionately on the back and grinned at Hopper. Joni ignored them and began to worm his way through the opening in the rubble into the side of the car.

"There'd be loads of room in here if we took the seats out," he began, his voice sounding muffled, but then the others heard a yelp of alarm as he backed hastily out.

"What happened? What's in there?" asked Karim.

"I don't know. Something's alive. Something moved. I thought it might be—you know—a snake or something."

"A snake? In the middle of Ramallah? It couldn't be," scoffed Hopper, but he made no move to look into the car himself.

And then something wholly unexpected happened. With a strident meow, a tabby cat, lean and rangy with its tail erect, streaked up from behind them and disappeared into the car.

"The snake doesn't stand much of a chance against the cat," said Karim.

They stood silently and watched. There was a clattering sound as if something metallic had been dislodged and then, unmistakably, the high-pitched mewing of a kitten.

"She's got her babies in there," said Joni, sounding relieved. "That's what must have been moving."

Karim crawled cautiously through to the side of the car and looked in. The cat lay curled on the back seat with one—no, two kittens snuggled up against her. She raised her head and bared her teeth at him, but made no attempt to attack. "Good for you," he said soothingly. "Yeah. You stay there. Good for you."

He liked the idea of the cats. Their presence gave the old car a new status. It was a good place for them, safe and secret, a place to hide.

Joni was enthusiastically heaving pieces of broken cinder block off the pile that was obscuring the front of the car.

"Wait, stop," said Karim, putting out a restraining hand.

"What's the matter?" said Joni.

"Don't you see? If we left this stuff here, and built it up a bit more even, the car would be hidden. Anyone coming here would think there was just a pile of rubbish, but we could make it so that there'd be a secret way in."

"Good," Hopper said succinctly. "I like that."

"A place to hide from *them*," said Joni approvingly.

Hopper walked up and down in front of the pile of rubble, surveying its possibilities. Joni scrambled up till he was standing on the roof of the car and looked out across the whole area.

"Karim's right," he called out to Hopper. "Come up here."

The other two climbed up after him, snagging their clothes on old coiled bedsprings and watching out for broken glass. They stepped gingerly on to the roof of the car, afraid that the metal might buckle under their combined weight.

Karim was used to the outlook from the steep hillsides of Ramallah, but the sweep of the view in front of him seemed almost new. The rocky, dry hillsides of Palestine glowed golden and ivory under the afternoon sun. New buildings rose up everywhere, and gashes in the brown earth showed where more were planned. A few old olive trees stood in the remnants of forgotten groves, their silky grey-green leaves shimmering in the breeze. Here and there a fig tree still clung to the wall of an ancient terrace, soon to be swept away in the creation of the new city. The sun, shining in from the west, slanted across from the lower, more fertile hills and plains of Israel that lay between Ramallah and the sea.

"What do you think, then?" Joni said, bringing Karim's attention back to the immediate surroundings.

Karim looked down. The rubble must have been tipped all around the car from the back of a dump truck. Peaks of it rose in waves, some higher than the roof of the car and some level with it. The car doors on the far side were still intact, and the rubble was banked right up against them so that they couldn't be opened.

There was a gap toward the front of the car, though, and it would still be possible to see through the windshield, which remained miraculously unbroken.

"We ought to cover the roof with something," Hopper said, "so that even if someone climbed up here they wouldn't see there was a car underneath."

"Yes, but what about letting the light in?" objected Karim. "If we dump stuff all over it, we'll cover up the windshield and it'll be dark inside."

Hopper didn't bother to answer. He'd jumped off the roof and was heaving at something on one of the mounds nearby. The other two clambered over to him, and saw that he was struggling to free an old broken shutter from a mass of heavy stones and concrete blocks which was pinning it down. They worked with him, enthusiastically heaving and tugging, ignoring their straining muscles and scratched hands. A few minutes later they stood triumphantly staring down at their find, then, slipping and stumbling on the loose stones, they managed to carry it back to the roof of the car.

They laid it down carefully.

"Hey," said Karim, "look at this. We can slide it backwards and forwards. If we're here and we need light inside, we can pull it back from the windshield end. When we go, or we want to hide it, we can just pull it forward again."

They tried it out. The shutter moved quite smoothly across the roof of the car and it covered the gap over the hood perfectly. As it grated over the metal roof, an angry meow of protest came from inside.

"We've scared her," said Karim. "She's going to have to get used to us, that's all."

"We'll bring them things to eat," said Joni. "Milk and bits of meat and stuff."

"Meat?" said Hopper incredulously. "You've got enough meat to spare for a cat?"

"My father's got a shop," Joni told him. "There's usually bits of meat that get too old to sell, that people can't eat. Cats wouldn't mind it, though."

From the refugee camp below came a crackling sound as the loudspeaker in the mosque was turned on and the first words of the evening call to prayer spilled out across the city.

"Is that the time?" Karim said. "It can't be."

He looked at Joni, then, shocked at what he'd seen, looked down at himself. Joni was doing the same. They were taking in the wreckage of their appearance, the smears of dirt and dust on their faces and hands and the filth sticking to their clothes. Joni saw that his uniform shirt was ripped from cuff to elbow, while Karim stared aghast at the jagged hole in the knee of his jeans.

"She'll kill me," they both said at the same time.

They laughed, and Karim was filled with a delicious sense of reckless happiness. He didn't care what was going to happen when he got home. It had been a good day. An amazing day, in fact.

"We've got to go," he said to Hopper, jumping down off the rubble. "See you tomorrow."

They were halfway up the hill above Hopper's ground when he remembered something.

"Hey, Joni," he said. "You'll never guess what. My stupid brother likes your sister. He wants a photo of her."

Joni stopped in his tracks and stared at Karim in disbelief.

"What?"

"I know. Sad, isn't it?"

"I mean, Violette, of all girls! Violette! And I always thought Jamal was kind of cool."

"Have you got one, then? A photo?"

"You'd better believe it. Loads of them. Violette's so dumb she gets herself photographed all the time. Leave it to me. No problem."

A load had rolled off Karim's shoulders. He held up his hand

105

and Joni slapped it. They'd come to the V in the road where their ways diverged.

"Tomorrow?" asked Karim with a lift of his eyebrows.

"Of course," said Joni, moving his bag from one shoulder to the other and setting off at a brisk trot for home.

Chapter Thirteen

The thunderous storm that broke over Karim's head when he crept into the apartment, hoping in vain to slip through the living room and into his own room unseen, was the worst he'd ever experienced. It began the moment he opened the front door.

"Karim!" his mother screeched. "Where exactly have you been? Don't you know what time it is? Don't you realize that I've been worried half out of my..."

She stopped, having taken in the full horror of his appearance.

"Oh, my darling! You've been caught in an explosion! Your clothes! Everything's torn to shreds! Are you hurt? Where were you hit?"

"I wasn't. I'm not. I've just been out, that's all," Karim said warily, trying to shrug her off.

She stared narrowly at him and her relief turned to fury.

"Out? And where's 'out'? What do you mean, 'out'? You're up to something. You've been getting into trouble. Karim, tell me. Where have you been? What have you been doing?"

Hassan Aboudi came out of the kitchen at that moment and joined in the inquisition. The tempest intensified and raged unabated for what seemed to Karim to be hours. Farah, her dark eyes snapping with pleasurable curiosity, abandoned her game with Sireen and watched closely. Sireen tugged at Lamia's trouser leg, hating the sound of the loud voices and hoping to be picked up.

It wasn't until Jamal arrived, walking unawares into the eye of the storm, that things began to ease. He stood inside the door, listening, then stepped forward.

"It's all right, Mama. Karim was out with Joni. I saw them. They were just playing around."

His parents' attention switched to him. The atmosphere cooled a little.

"With Joni? Why didn't he say so?"

Karim hunched a resentful shoulder.

"You didn't give me the chance to say a word."

"Don't speak to your mother in that tone of voice," snapped his father.

"If I were you," Jamal said lightly, daring a little laugh, "I wouldn't say anything at all."

His parents glared at him. Jamal spread out his hands placatingly.

"He's twelve, Baba. He's been in a fight, I bet. You won't get anything out of him. Why don't you send him off to have a shower? I can smell him from here. He's killing my appetite. What's it going to be, Mama? I thought I smelled meatballs."

Karim took his cue and bolted for the bathroom. He stripped off his clothes and stood under the shower, amazed at Jamal's cool brilliance, and deeply grateful. The water, sluicing down his body, was washing out more than the grit and grime of an eventful day. The terror on the rooftop had left a jagged residue in his mind, a kind of wound, but when he stepped out of the shower and toweled himself dry he felt almost healed. He realized that he was starving and very tired.

He picked up the bundle of dirty clothes on the bathroom floor, ready to dump them into the basket by the washing machine, and then he hesitated. Next time he went to Hopper's ground he'd probably get just as dirty. He couldn't face a fight like this every day.

I'll take some old clothes over there that Mama won't miss, he thought, and hide them in the car.

The cleverness of the idea made him feel good. He wrapped a towel around himself, dropped his dirty clothes in the basket and went to his bedroom.

"I owe you for that, Jamal," he said.

Jamal was writing something at the table. He didn't respond.

"I spoke to Joni," Karim went on. "He's going to get that photo for you."

Jamal whipped around.

"You didn't tell him why?"

"Course not." Karim had anticipated this. "I told him it was for a project on young people in Ramallah. For school."

"You're a good kid. Where were you this afternoon, anyway?"

Karim looked cautious.

"With Joni, like you said. You didn't actually see us?"

"No. It was a fair guess, though."

Karim hesitated. He wanted to tell Jamal about Hopper's fake bomb and the helicopter on the roof. Jamal would have been full of admiration, he knew. On the other hand, there were limits to brotherly trust. Next time Jamal wanted to get even, he'd probably tell their parents everything.

"Supper's ready!" Lamia called out, resolving his dilemma.

Karim scrambled into a clean white T-shirt and the brothers went into the kitchen, sitting down side by side at the table in a mood of rare harmony.

It wasn't until the next afternoon that Karim was able to slip off again. His mother had gone to the university very early, expecting long hold-ups at the Israeli checkpoint on the road, but Hassan Aboudi seemed in no hurry to go out too. He spread his accounts out on the big table in the living room and pored over them, his forehead creased with worry.

"Is the shop still closed, Baba?" Karim asked timidly.

"Until later on this morning. I'll be getting a delivery in then. Come to think of it, since you've got nothing better to do, you can come down and help me. There's still a lot of cleaning up to do."

Karim bit his lip, annoyed with himself.

In the end, though, he quite enjoyed helping out in the shop. The worst of the mess had been cleared up and the stock was beginning to look good again, the microwave ovens, irons, fans and blenders gleaming on the shelves. The delivery had miraculously arrived, in spite of all the expected obstacles, and Hassan Aboudi's black mood lifted for a while as he made room for the new items, unpacking one or two for display and stowing the remainder tidily at the back of the shop.

"You can hop along now, Karim," he said at last. "No more fighting, OK?" And he actually squeezed Karim's shoulders in an understanding hug, which made Karim feel guilty, confused and affectionate all at the same time.

From under the counter, he retrieved the plastic bag containing the worn old clothes, which he had secreted there on his arrival, and tore off. It was so late that Joni must have been out of school for ages by now. He'd have been down at Hopper's ground for hours already.

When he arrived, breathless from having run all the way, he thought at first that the place was deserted. He looked around, disappointed, then heard murmuring coming from where the car was buried in the mound of rubble. Carefully, so as not to dirty the favorite faded jeans he was wearing, he wormed his way between the rubbish until he was looking in through the side of the car.

Joni was crouching inside it alone. He was dangling a strip of meat in front of one of the kittens, who was trying to snatch at it with outstretched paws. The mother, wary but unafraid, lay licking herself, reclining against the back seat in luxurious ease.

"They're so cool, these kittens," Joni said, looking up briefly at

Karim. "This one's the liveliest. I'm calling him Ginger. There's another one, a little one that's really weak. I've tried to feed her but she doesn't take it easily."

Karim watched as Ginger hooked the strip of meat on the point of a sharp little claw, twitching it out of Joni's fingers. He shifted his weight, afraid of getting a cramp.

"I've got to change," he said. "I brought some old clothes. Mama had a fit when she saw me last night."

He wriggled back away from the car. Joni followed him.

"So did mine. You would have thought I'd committed some awful crime. Murder or something. Good idea to bring some old clothes. I wish I'd thought of it."

"I'm going to leave them here. Hide them in the car."

Joni nodded.

"Cool. I'll do that too."

"Where's Hopper?"

"I don't know. He didn't come."

Karim looked around, needing a place to change. It wasn't hard to find one. The mountains of rubble along the edge of Hopper's ground had plenty of angles where he could hide without a risk of being seen. He emerged a moment later in a faded old T-shirt and some old combat trousers of Jamal's that he knew would never be missed. Joni was pulling something out of his schoolbag.

"What's that?" asked Karim.

"A photo. Of my sister. Like you wanted."

He sounded doubtful.

"Here, let's see."

Karim took the photo out of Joni's unwilling hand and burst out laughing.

"You've got to be joking!"

The photo was a soft-focus studio shot. Violette was posed against a rose-covered arch. Her head was tilted to one side and her cheek was resting on her hand. She was gazing soulfully into the camera. It was perfect, exactly the sort of romantic garbage that Jamal would probably love, except for one thing. Someone had scribbled a mustache on Violette's upper lip and drawn a crude pair of glasses around her eyes.

"I thought it would be super-easy," Joni said. "Like I told you, there are millions of pictures of Violette. The only thing was, I'd forgotten that she and her stupid friends have this craze for albums. They stick everything into them. I hunted high and low, I promise you, and this photo was the only one not in an album that I could find, except for all the framed ones Mama's stuck around the apartment, and I could hardly take one of those, could I?"

"Who did the glasses and stuff?"

"Me." Joni looked embarrassed. "It was months ago. I was mad, and I just grabbed a marker and did it."

"It's a marker then, not a ball point pen?" Karim held the photo up to his eyes and scrutinized it closely.

"Yes."

"Well, it might rub off. Marker doesn't stick well on this shiny paper. He sat down on a stone, put Joni's bag on his knee and rested the photo on it. Then he licked his finger and began to rub at the mustache.

"You're rubbing out the picture," said Joni, staring critically over his shoulder.

"Only a bit. It's coming off, look."

He held the photo up. There was a slightly odd look now to Violette's mouth, a black shadow on her upper lip, as if she was a man who hadn't shaved for a while, but it was definitely an improvement.

Karim began to work on the glasses. Joni, in the first flush of his rage, had pressed harder here. The black marks were coming away, but more of the photo was too. Violette now looked a little owl-like, with grey rings and white rub marks circling her eyes. The effect was odd, though it was hard to say quite why.

112

"We could touch it up a bit maybe, to get the color right," said Joni, reaching into his bag. He pulled out his pencil case and gave it to Karim.

Karim selected a cream-colored crayon and began to work over the erased areas. His tongue, flickering at the corner of his mouth, showed his concentration. He finished at last, and held the photo up for Joni's approval.

"If you hold it away, and half shut your eyes," said Joni, "it sort of looks OK."

Karim nodded.

"It's a photo anyway. It's obviously Violette. What more does the fool want? Thanks a million, Joni. You've saved my life. I can get Lineman back now."

Footsteps made them turn. Hopper was coming towards them.

"Hi," he said shortly.

"Hello," said Karim. He nearly added, "Where have you been?" but Hopper's face was closed and set, repelling curiosity.

"Aren't we going to get started?" Hopper said, looking at the others disapprovingly, as if he'd expected transformations to have taken place by now.

"Doing what?" asked Joni.

Hopper didn't answer. He stood tensely with his arms crossed, looking around. The others, bereft of ideas, waited.

"We should make our base safer, hide it more," Hopper said at last. "This way they'd find it easily if they came to look for us."

"Conceal the entrance, you mean?" said Karim.

He was looking at an old oil drum as he spoke. He walked across to it and peered inside. It was half filled with earth and stones. He pushed at it, but it didn't move.

"Come and help me, you two," he called over his shoulder. "We can roll it if we tip it over."

They heaved the drum onto its side and rolled it towards the car.

"If we get it upright again," said Karim, "we could bank stuff around it and get a whole lot more things, and make a sort of passageway, with a kink in it, running up to the place where you crawl into the car. You'd only see how to get in if you came right up and looked closely."

Joni's mind was leaping ahead.

"We need a few more drums. Two or three at least."

"Not in a row, though," objected Karim. "They'd look too obvious."

He was already bounding over to another oil drum that was lying on its side, half buried under loose earth. He was pulling at the top of it, trying to shift it. The others went to help him. They tugged at it, and showers of dust and small stones spattered them as the oil drum suddenly came free, then they arranged it artistically to hide the entrance to the car.

"That's so good," Joni said. "We just need one more—"

"Not now," said Karim impatiently. "Where's the ball? Let's play."

Hopper picked up Joni's wrist to look at his watch.

"I can't stay long. I'll have to go in a minute."

"Why?" Joni sounded disappointed.

"My mother needs me," Hopper said awkwardly.

The other two said nothing.

"She went to Jerusalem today," Hopper said, "to visit my brother Salim."

"What's he doing in Jerusalem?" asked Joni.

"He's in prison. In al-Muskobiya."

Karim shuddered. Everyone knew of the tortures inflicted on Palestinian prisoners in the notorious Israeli prison.

"When did they take him?" asked Joni.

"A month ago." Hopper took a deep breath. "Me and Salim were at a checkpoint. This soldier, a woman, she told Salim to show his ID. It was pouring and the ground was all wet and muddy. Anyway, he gave his card to her and she just held it out and dropped it in the mud. Then she told him to pick it up."

Karim's jaw tightened with anger.

"Did he?"

"No. You don't know Salim." Hopper spoke with a mixture of pride and regret. "He just turned his head away."

"So what happened?"

"She said, 'Pick it up,' and he didn't, didn't move at all. I was so scared. I knew something bad would happen. She went on saying, 'Pick it up or you'll see what you get,' like she was really enjoying it. Really loving her power. In the end, Salim did. He had to, or his card would have gotten soaked through and been useless. I thought it was all over, and we started walking away, but this soldier, she went to another one, a man, and spoke to him, and he looked at Salim and shouted, 'You, come here!' and he took his card and said, 'It's impossible to read this. It's covered in mud. It's not valid any more. Go back. You can't go through.' And then it was awful. It was so awful."

Hopper's voice trembled and he dashed his sleeve across his eyes. Karim didn't know what to do. Hopper had always seemed so tough before. Karim wanted to say something, but he couldn't find the words.

"Salim's got this temper," Hopper went on. "When he gets going—he was beginning to lose it, I could tell. He grabbed the Israeli's arm and started shaking it and shouting. So two more of them came running, and they got him in an armlock and pushed him down to the ground, and he just looked up at me and said, 'Look after Mama. Don't get into trouble.'"

"They took him away. It took Mama till last week to find out where he was. It was the first time she'd tried to visit him today. She started out at six o'clock this morning, and got through the checkpoints all right, got to Jerusalem and everything, and they kept her waiting till two—six hours—and then said she couldn't see him, she had to go home. She's been crying and crying. I just wanted to get away for a bit, so I came here, but I'll have to go back now. She's always scared I'll get arrested too."

"She's right, with you planting fake bombs and stuff," said Karim, to lighten the atmosphere.

Hopper grinned.

"My little bit of personal revenge."

Joni picked up his schoolbag.

"We won't go on doing things here without you," he said. "We'll wait till we can all do stuff together."

Karim swallowed his disappointment. He'd been looking forward to a long session of planning and building.

"Yes, OK. Joni's right," he said.

Hopper hesitated. Then he looked away and said, "I wish you'd come and see her. See Mama, I mean. She's scared I'm hanging out with some of the hard kids from the camp. She thinks I'm going to get involved in heavy stuff. Real bombings. It would be good if she could meet you."

"Oh, so we're just a couple of softies," said Joni.

Hopper's face went blank.

"It's OK. You don't have to come. Sorry I said anything."

He turned to go.

"No, we will, of course we will," Karim said hastily. "Hang on a minute while I change and hide my things."

He dived into his changing place and came out a moment later in his good clothes. He crawled carefully into the car, murmured soothingly to the cat, hid the bundle of old clothes under the front seat, and wriggled out again.

"Cool idea, keeping stuff here," said Hopper approvingly. "Come on. Let's go."

Chapter Fourteen

The metal door at the front of the little stone house was ajar and Hopper pushed it further open, kicking off his shoes to leave them on the step outside. Karim and Joni followed shyly.

They'd entered a small living room with plain whitewashed walls. A sofa, bright with embroidered cushions, ran the length of one wall, and two big armchairs and a low coffee table, on which stood a small display of artificial flowers, used up most of the rest of the space. An old man was sitting on one of the chairs. His head was covered with a snowy-white keffiyeh, which was held in place by two circles of black rope. His eyes were bright and sharp against the weathered, wrinkled skin of his nut brown face. He had been staring down at the floor, his hands resting on the head of his stick, but when the boys came in he looked up and his face brightened.

"*Ya*, Sami," he said, looking at Hopper.

"Sami?" thought Karim, surprised. That must be Hopper's real name.

He looked at Hopper again. Having an ordinary name made him seem younger somehow.

Hopper bent down to kiss his grandfather.

"These are my friends, *sidi*," he said. "Karim and Joni."

"You are very welcome." The old man waved a hand. "Sit down. Sit down."

Hopper disappeared through an open doorway. Karim and Joni, sitting tongue-tied on the edge of the sofa, heard the clatter of dishes and murmur of voices beyond, then Hopper reappeared with his mother following. Karim recognized the woman carrying the sack who had called out to him before. She showed no sign of remembering him. Her eyes were red and her face was heavy with exhaustion, but she summoned up a smile.

"This is Joni. He goes to a private school," Hopper said, trying to impress her. "And Karim. He's my friend from our school. He lives on the other side of town. He gets really good marks for everything."

Karim wriggled with embarrassment. He could hardly believe the transformation that had come over Hopper. The daring, free-spirited boy had been replaced by a dutiful, respectful son. He seemed to have shrunk, to have become younger and smaller.

Hopper's mother pulled a few coins out of her pocket and passed them to him with a murmured instruction. He darted out of the main door and a few minutes later was back with a clutch of soda bottles in each hand. He opened them with a flick of the bottle opener lying on the table and passed them around. Karim and Joni drank gratefully, suddenly aware of their thirst.

"Is that Salim?" asked Karim, looking up at a framed picture hanging high on the wall, just below the ceiling. It showed a slim-faced young man with a serious expression.

"No. It's an old one. It's my father," said Hopper.

The old man sighed and shook his head.

"Peace be upon him."

Joni and Karim exchanged looks, feeling uncomfortable. Hopper's mother sighed heavily.

"It was one year ago, almost exactly," she said.

"He went to Kuwait to find work," Hopper explained gruffly. "There was nothing for him here. He used to send us money. That was how we managed to move out of the camp into this place. But there was an accident at the building site where he worked. We never found out exactly what happened."

Tears, which seemed to have been held back only by the boys' arrival, began to slide gently down his mother's face, and Hopper's grandfather leaned across and patted her hand.

"Karim's really good at soccer, Mama," Hopper said hastily. "We've been playing together."

His mother wiped her eyes and smiled.

"Good. Very good. You boys keep out of trouble. One son in prison is enough."

Joni's eyes had been wandering around the room, sliding over the picture of the Al Aqsa mosque in Jerusalem and the framed motto which read, in scarlet cross-stitch, "God Bless Our Home." They had come to a rest on a large old key hanging from a nail.

Hopper's grandfather saw what he was looking at.

"That's the key to our house," he said, nodding.

Joni glanced sideways at the metal door. The key looked too heavy and old-fashioned to fit it.

"Not this house," the old man said. "Our house in Ramle."

Joni looked surprised.

"But Ramle's in Israel," he said. "I thought they didn't allow us to go there."

The grandfather's eyes snapped.

"What they allow! What they don't allow! I remember, to this day, exactly how they drove us out. More than fifty years ago, but I can see it like yesterday. Panic, terror, guns firing everywhere. We were the lucky ones. So many others were shot. My mother locked the door of our house as we left and gave me the key. 'Look after it,' she said. 'We'll be back soon. A few weeks, maybe, when things have calmed down.'

"How could she possibly know that they'd take our house and everything in it, and never let us go home again?"

A red flush was suffusing his face. He seemed about to explode, but he caught Hopper's eye, stopped and shook his head. "Well, boys, so you're soccer players, are you? That's good. Palestine for the World Cup, eh?"

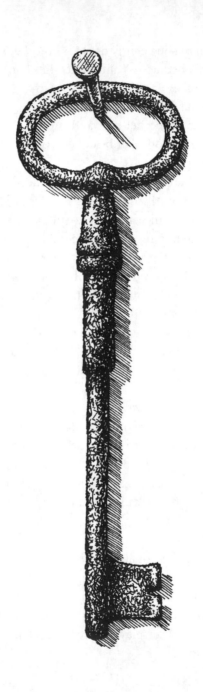

Everyone laughed, glad that the tension had been relieved.

"Thank you," Hopper said a few minutes later, when they'd left the house and were skirting his mother's neatly laid-out vegetable patch towards the road. "Meeting you cheered them up, I could tell. They're really upset about Salim, and they keep going on and on about how worried they are whenever I'm not there."

"You can't exactly blame them, when you go around pretending to blow things up," said Joni.

Hopper grinned sheepishly. Karim wasn't listening. He was thinking about Hopper's family and the awful things that had happened to them.

"I'm sorry about your father, dying like that in Kuwait," he said awkwardly.

He was wondering how he would manage if Baba had died and Jamal was in prison. The very idea was making him shudder.

Hopper's really, really brave, he thought admiringly.

"Is it just you and Salim in your family?" said Joni, taking a tissue from his pocket to wipe a sticky drip of soda from his chin. "You haven't got any more brothers and sisters?"

"I've got a sister. Muna. She's married. She lives in the camp." Hopper jerked his chin towards the warren of jumbled buildings and narrow, overcrowded lanes further down the hill.

"Was that really the key to your house in Ramle?" Karim asked curiously.

"Yes. And we're going to keep it forever, till they let us go back to our old house again." Hopper sounded fierce.

"The Israelis will never let the refugees go back home, though," said Karim, then wished he hadn't.

Hopper didn't answer, but squared his shoulders defiantly.

I'm glad I'm not a refugee, thought Karim. He'd never wondered before what it must have been like for the people in the camp.

Joni said, "I've got to go home. My father's fixed some extra math lessons for me. The teacher's coming this evening."

They said goodbye to Hopper and began to walk quickly back into town. Neither of them was in the mood for talking.

"Thanks for the photo," Karim said, when they came to parting ways.

"You can have the original any time you like," said Joni. "Sisters were deliberately put on earth to torture brothers. I know this."

"You're right," said Karim, thinking of Farah. "You are so right."

Farah and Rasha were playing in the girls' bedroom when he arrived home. He could hear their high excited voices as they tried to cajole Sireen into wearing something or doing something that she clearly didn't like.

"Is Jamal at home?" he said to his mother as casually as he could.

She gave him a sharp look.

"Yes. Where have you been?"

"With Joni," Karim said virtuously. "We were doing—artwork with photographs."

"Artwork?" Lamia looked surprised. "I didn't know you were interested in... "

But Karim had already gone into his room and shut the door behind him.

All the way home, he had been hugging himself with pleasure at the thought of presenting the photograph to Jamal. He'd been preening himself on his cleverness, looking forward to Jamal's praise and, above all, to the return of Lineman. But now that Jamal's moody, handsome face was right there in front of him, now that Jamal was staring up at him with a sardonic lift to his eyebrows, Karim didn't feel quite so confident. The retouched photo, with the rubbed bits round the eyes and upper lip, might be worse than he remembered. Jamal might think he was being cheeky or something.

"I've got something for you," he said, as nonchalantly as he could, reaching into the inner pocket of his bomber jacket.

Jamal had been lying on his bed, but he sat up with a jerk.

"You've got it? Let me see."

With a flourish that disguised his uncertainty, Karim produced the photo and put it into Jamal's hands. Then he stepped back out of reach and waited.

Jamal took the photo reverently and gazed down at it. Expressions of delight, puzzlement, disappointment and suspicion chased each other across his face.

"Someone's been drawing on this."

"Photographer touched it up I expect. They do that sometimes."

"It's like—sort of ghostly glasses around her eyes."

"Really? Let's see."

Karim twitched the photo out of Jamal's fingers and pretended to scrutinize it.

"Na. Trick of the light. Nice background, isn't it?"

Jamal took the photo back and glanced at Karim with narrowed eyes.

"Hey!" Karim spread out his hands. "Don't I get any thanks? It's what you wanted, isn't it? A photo of Violette, you said. This is a photo of Violette, if I'm not mistaken. Looking pretty gorgeous, if you ask me. How about, 'Oh, thank you, Karim. You are such a good guy. I'll get Lineman back for you immediately. I'm just putting my coat on and I'll go out and fetch it now?'"

"Hm. There's a bit rubbed off here. On her lip."

"Whose lip? What are you talking about?"

Both brothers spun around. Farah had pushed open the door and was staring at them. Jamal thrust the photograph under a book on the table. Farah noticed, and a smile curled her mouth. Karim advanced on her.

"If we ever catch you in here again, you sneaky little troublemaker, your dolls will be spending the rest of their little lives in the hospital for legless toys."

Farah's mouth opened and a wail began to emerge from it.

"Shut it," Jamal said loftily. "Out. Now."

Wordlessly, Farah backed out of the room, closing the door behind her with a quiet, fearful click.

Jamal sat down at the table, propped the photo in front of him and gazed at it. His expression, to Karim's disgusted eye, was soulful.

It's worked, then, he told himself. He likes it after all.

"Lineman," he said jauntily. "Lineman, Lineman, Lineman."

"I heard you." Jamal didn't move. "Soon. I promise. Now get off my back, OK?"

Chapter Fifteen

School reopened two days later. The rooms still smelled of new concrete and fresh putty, and a layer of dust and grit had settled over everything. The science labs had been completely wrecked, so that all the timetables had had to be altered, and the loss of the school's computers meant that the office, with all its records gone, was in chaos. Lessons, however, were starting up again, with everyone managing as best as they could.

"Why does school have to be so *boring*?" Karim asked himself for the hundredth time, as he sat at a splintered table in the classroom, looking out the window, only half aware of Mr. Mohammed's voice droning on.

He came to with a start as a sharp blow connected with the back of his head.

"Karim Aboudi!" Mr. Mohammed had sneaked up unheard and was standing over him. He took a handful of Karim's hair and forced his head back. Karim was looking directly up into Mr. Mohammed's unpleasant face, at the hairs growing out of his gaping nostrils and the red veins running in networks across the whites of his eyes.

"Copy! Copy! You have to copy what I've written on the board! Why haven't you opened your book? Why haven't you picked up your pen? Are you lazy or stupid? Are you deaf? What are you?"

"Sorry, *ya ustaz*," murmured Karim.

He felt the painful grip on his hair lessen and dared to reach out for his pen. Mr. Mohammed let him go and stalked back to his desk on the dais in front of the class. With a sigh, Karim began to copy.

The morning passed with mind-numbing slowness. Karim did as he was told, copying, writing exercises, taking notes—trying as best as he could to avoid the eye of the teachers, who, strained and anxious as they were, seemed more inclined than usual to threaten severe punishments for any lapse of attention or infringement of the rules. He'd been beaten before. He didn't want it to happen again.

It was hard to concentrate, though. He gazed vacantly out the window, ignoring the drone of Mr. Mohammed's voice, the book on the desk in front of him forgotten.

An explosion somewhere unpleasantly close brought his head up with a jerk. The familiar electricity of fear crisped his stomach and set his hair on end. The children sitting near the window had dropped automatically to the floor and were crawling towards the classroom's inner wall, frightened of flying shards of glass. Wasim, a thin boy who seldom spoke, had shot to his feet and was standing rigid, perfectly still, whimpering in a high, terrified voice.

The classroom door opened and the school secretary looked in. "They're moving away, towards the refugee camp. Message from the principal. No one's to leave the school without permission." He stopped, and looked at Wasim, his face softening. "It's all right, *habibi*. There's no danger around here."

The children on the floor stood up cautiously and drifted back to their desks. Wasim had stopped whimpering and was biting his lips, staring straight ahead. Mr. Mohammed maneuvered between the desks and touched his arm. Karim didn't listen to what he was murmuring. Wasim always went funny when he heard shooting or explosions. Something had happened to his father, but he wasn't sure what. Everyone was used to him now.

The aftermath of fear was working itself out. The children were edgy and restless. Mr. Mohammed went back to his desk at the front of the classroom.

"Settle down," he barked. "We'll start from the beginning again. Look at page twenty-three. The questions at the bottom... "

Nobody was paying attention. Eyes kept turning towards the windows. Ears were pricked for further sounds outside.

Mr. Mohammed, whose own hands were shaking, reacted as usual by losing his temper.

"Read it! Read!" he stormed to the luckless boy he'd picked on. "Are you stupid or ignorant, or both? You think we haven't wasted enough time already? If any of you get an education worth speaking of, it'll be a miracle. Forget what's going on out there and concentrate."

Hypocrite, thought Karim, looking sourly at his teacher. He's scared himself. That's why he picks on us. Why can't we have a decent teacher like Jamal's?

He thought of Mr. Bashir as he'd seen him in the corridor that morning, surrounded by a knot of students, their faces expectant and purposeful.

He pretended to look down at his book, but the words seemed to jump about. The shock that had bolted through him at the sound of the explosion had left everything jangling in its wake.

He let his mind drift away to Hopper's ground. The thought of it calmed and reassured him. Once they'd cleared a good-sized open space for soccer, they'd be able to play actual games, real ones, get other kids to make up a team, and organize matches. It would be their own place. They'd be in charge of it themselves.

Unconsciously, his feet began to shift across the dusty classroom floor as he imagined himself playing a game there. Now he was running down the field, passing to a midfielder, on into the penalty area, taking the ball again, dodging around a defender, the ball at his feet a part of himself, an extension of himself, and—yes! Into the goal!

The class around him was beginning to relax, but Karim was far away, walking triumphantly off the field, raising his arms to acknowledge the cheers of the crowd, and smiling modestly into the lenses of the TV cameras.

He licked his lips. All that running had made him thirsty—or perhaps it was, after all, the dust that was swirling through the partially repaired school. At any rate, it was making him think. They were always getting thirsty at Hopper's ground. He'd ask Joni to get some soft drinks from his father. They could keep them in the car. Later, in the summer, they could even rig up a shady place in one corner, a place like a little café, with somewhere nice to sit. That would be good. That would make their presence more permanent, somehow.

As Hopper was in a different class, Karim rarely saw him during the course of the school day, but at noon, when the morning shift of children left, ready for the afternoon shift to come in, they exploded out through the school gate together.

Usually, they walked side by side, but today Hopper sprinted ahead.

"Wait for me!" Karim called after him.

Hopper's pace didn't slacken. Karim put on a spurt and caught up with him.

"What's the matter with you? What's the hurry?"

Hopper's expression, as he turned to Karim, was almost a snarl.

"The shooting! They said it was coming from the camp."

Karim felt stupid. He'd been relieved when he'd realized that the trouble had been nowhere near home. He hadn't thought how it would be for Hopper.

They raced on together, expecting at every corner to come face to face with a tank or an armored vehicle, to hear a shouted order or the revving of a heavy engine. Nothing happened. The road was clear.

Hopper turned into the little path that led through his mother's vegetable patch. His grandfather was standing outside, talking to another old man.

"We heard shooting while we were at school," Hopper panted. "They said there was trouble at the camp. What's happened, *sidi*?"

His grandfather shifted his weight painfully from one arthritic hip to the other.

"It's over. They were making arrests. They've taken Tarik Zuhair and Ali Fouad, and some others. Rounding people up. Tank shells blasting into people's homes. Five people injured. No one killed for once, thank God."

"Muna's all right?"

"Yes. Your sister's fine. Your mother's been to see her." He turned back to the other man. "That would be Yousuf's son you were telling me about. Now, his brother... "

The old men's voices faded away as Hopper and Karim walked slowly back towards the road.

"How's your brother doing?" Karim asked. "Is there any news of him?"

Hopper shook his head.

"Not much. It's hard to find anything out. I've got an uncle in Jerusalem. He keeps going to the prison, in case someone's released and can tell him something. But he's got a job, and he hasn't got much time to spare."

There was a short silence.

"I wish we could get in there, into al-Muskobiya, and help Salim escape," said Karim. "You know, like in a James Bond film."

He pretended to hold a gun at hip level, swiveling it around and making shooting noises.

Hopper laughed bitterly.

"I've got this awful feeling," he said, "that something bad's going to happen to him. That he'll die in there and I'll never see him again."

Chapter Sixteen

The boys were subdued as they entered Hopper's ground. Karim retrieved the ball from the car and kicked it to Hopper, but Hopper merely trapped it under his foot and sat down on the big stone that formed the last major obstruction in the middle of the space they'd painstakingly cleared. He had withdrawn into his own thoughts and Karim didn't know what to say.

A meow made them turn their heads. The cat had appeared. She rubbed herself against Hopper's shin, then leapt lightly onto the big stone and sat beside him. Delicately, she lifted a forepaw and began to lick the white fur on her belly.

Hopper murmured to her as he gently stroked her head. The cat seemed almost to listen for a moment, then she arched her neck and rubbed the side of her face against his hand. Watching them, Karim had an odd sense that they understood each other. As if she could read his thoughts, the cat gave Hopper's hand several rasping licks, then began to purr. He smiled, and stroked her under her chin.

They're both—I don't know—sort of wild, thought Karim.

He felt oddly jealous.

"Where are the kittens?" he said out loud. "I didn't see them in the car."

"They're growing up," Hopper said, sounding superior, as if he had expert knowledge. "Maybe they're off exploring somewhere."

Joni arrived, out of breath. He threw his schoolbag down on the ground and Hopper stood up to let him sit on the stone.

"There's a load of trouble in town," Joni said. "More arrests. Israelis everywhere. I nearly didn't get here."

"They were firing tank shells into the camp," said Karim, looking sideways at Hopper.

Automatically, as they so often did without being aware of it, they lifted their heads to listen, their faces tightening as tension rippled through them. Then Joni bent to retrieve his schoolbag. He fished a squashy plastic bag out of it, and upended it, tipping a tangle of raw chickens' heads and gizzards onto the dusty ground. With a squeak, the cat jumped down, sniffed the pile over, chose a crushed head and began to crunch her way through it. Then she picked out a gizzard and trotted purposefully away with it towards the rubble.

"Party time for kittens," said Joni.

She was back a moment later. She made straight for Hopper and coiled around his leg, purring loudly.

"It's me you should be thanking, not him," objected Joni. "Who brought you all those chicky bits, eh?"

Hopper smiled delightedly, looking suddenly younger.

"She likes me best, don't you, Aziza?"

"Aziza?" queried Karim.

"Yes, that's her name."

"She told you, I suppose." Karim felt absurdly irritated.

Hopper didn't answer. Aziza picked up another piece of chicken and carried it away.

"Come on," Karim said impatiently. "Are we going to play soccer or what?"

He began to jump around, like a sub at a big match warming up on the sidelines. The others moved slowly away from the big stone. He could sense that they weren't in the mood to play today. In his heart of hearts, he wasn't either.

Hopper kicked the ball to Joni and with a sluggish tap Joni kicked it back. Karim watched, his spirits drooping. Then the ball came suddenly towards him and he lunged a savage kick at it. It shot off further and faster than he'd intended and landed on the pile of rubble, out of sight.

"Idiot," Joni said good-humoredly, beginning to climb up after it. "Flat-footed oaf."

Karim's mood was worsening. Everything seemed wrong.

Hopper had drifted over to the rubble pile to look for Aziza and the kittens. Karim stared out over the space they'd cleared.

What's the point of all this? he thought. This place—it's nothing. There's nothing here. And I can't even kick straight anymore.

The ball suddenly bounced towards him. He caught it and looked up to see Joni clattering down from the pile of rubble, holding a can in each hand.

"Look what I've found," he called out, waving to them triumphantly.

"Wow. Big deal. Cans," Karim said nastily.

Joni hooked his toes around Karim's ankle in an attempt to tip him over. Karim kept his balance with difficulty and turned on him. Joni was thrusting a can into his face.

"Paint. Green and red paint. There's lots left inside. Listen."

He shook the cans to make the liquid slosh around.

Hopper had come back.

"Paint? Let's see."

"I can't get the lid off," said Joni. "I tried. But you can tell the colors by the drips down the side."

He pulled a penknife from his pocket, put the blade under the lip of the lid and tried to pry it off.

"Careful. You'll snap it," said Karim. "Give it to me."

He took the knife from Joni, snapped the cutting blade shut and selected the screwdriver. The lid came off after a brief struggle and the boys looked down into a pool of bright, viscous green.

"It's awesome," breathed Joni.

"It's fantastic," said Hopper.

They opened the other can. The red was even better than the green. It glowed as bright as poppies, as shiny as blood.

"Too bad there isn't any black or white," Karim said. "We could have made a Palestinian flag."

"How? We haven't got anything to paint a flag onto," said Joni.

"Yes, we have." Karim was beginning to feel excited. "The wall at the back. A flag would look great there."

"But we haven't got any black or white," said Joni, bringing the discussion back to point zero again.

Hopper was watching Aziza, who had returned to lick the last bits of chicken juice from the plastic bag in which Joni had brought the scraps.

"We could do a flag," he said slowly, "if we use loose stones. We could paint some, and wrap the others in black or white plastic bags. We could just lay them out on the ground."

The others gaped at him.

"Hopper, that's so cool," said Joni.

"It's brilliant," said Karim.

Galvanized at last, they shot off in different directions to collect stones and a few minutes later had amassed a good pile.

"We haven't got any paintbrushes," said Joni.

"Don't need them," said Hopper. "Wait here."

He dashed away towards the rubble and a moment later had come back carrying an old hubcap. He laid it on the ground, where it made a wide, shallow bowl. He tipped some green paint into it, dipped the first stone and set it down on the ground to dry.

"Let me try," said Karim.

They took turns. The results were deeply satisfying. By the time the paint ran out, eighteen stones were a brilliant, glossy green.

"You've got it all over your shoes," Joni said to Karim.

"So? It's all over your hands," Karim retorted. "And on your chin."

Hopper had fetched another buckled hubcap and was already tipping red paint into it. They had to work more carefully this time. There was less paint in the red can and it was thicker. To make it go further, they smeared it on the stones with the corner of an old torn curtain, then used the rest of the cloth to try, unsuccessfully, to clean themselves up.

"You two look awful," Joni giggled. "You're covered in it."

"I don't care," said Hopper.

"I do. She'll kill me," said Karim.

He was already looking around, though, for the black and white plastic they'd need to finish the flag.

There was always plenty of torn plastic fluttering around the rubble. It took only a few moments to collect a good amount.

They arranged the green stones in a long strip and put a white stripe beside it. Two big black bin liners, emptied out, provided enough plastic to cover the stones needed to make the third stripe. The red stones, artistically arranged, formed the triangle at one end of the flag.

When it was done, they stood and gazed at their handiwork. It was spectacular, much better than they had expected. They walked around it, admiring it from different angles.

"We could have made it even bigger," said Karim, nudging into place a white stone that hadn't been aligned to his satisfaction.

"I think it's perfect just like it is," said Joni. "Salim will love this, when he gets out," said Hopper. Karim's mood had changed completely. He felt a swelling pride, a new confidence. They'd done something here, on this little piece of ground. They'd made it truly theirs.

Chapter Seventeen

The television set was on as usual, a bright eye shining out of a dark corner of the living room, next to a tall potted plant, which leaned over, threatening to obscure it. The news had come on.

Israeli soldiers entered a refugee camp in Gaza this morning. Three Palestinians, including an eight-year-old boy, were killed. One Israeli soldier was wounded. In a separate incident, tanks entered the town of Jenin and demolished three houses belonging to suspected militants. An elderly woman was crushed to death when she did not evacuate the house in time.

Why is the news always bad? thought Karim, feeling the familiar tension fasten its hand around his stomach. Why doesn't anything good ever happen to us?

He was on his hands and knees, fishing under the sofa for his pen, which had rolled just out of reach. Above his head he could almost hear the heavy, despairing silence of his parents as they listened to the announcer's measured voice, and then the wailing sound of relatives as the camera cut to yet another funeral.

He stretched his arm to its limit and just managed to curl his slender fingers around his pen. The sofa was too low for him to get a proper grip on it. He began to roll it towards him, inch by inch.

"They won't be satisfied until they've driven us out of our

whole country and taken all of it for themselves," Hassan Aboudi burst out. "I tell you, Lamia...."

Karim stopped listening. His pen had rolled out into the open. He picked it up, went to his room and shut the door. He was going to put in half an hour—an hour even—of solid work before he went out to Hopper's ground. If he was ever going to get anywhere in life, he would have to start getting serious about schoolwork. Exams would have to be passed.

He worked diligently for an hour, sitting at the table surrounded by books, his tongue flickering at the corner of his mouth as he wrote. Then, with a sigh of relief, he dropped his pen, stood up and tiptoed to the door. The best way to get out of the apartment was to take his parents by surprise, before they had time to think up an objection. He opened the door cautiously, then slipped silently out of his room. The living room was empty now, but his parents' voices came from the kitchen.

"I'm just going to see Joni," he said, sticking his head around the kitchen door and withdrawing it quickly, but before he could slide away, his mother looked up and said sharply, "Oh, no, you don't. You're staying right here."

"What? I can't, Mama. Joni's promised to help me with my math. He said... "

A frown was settling on his father's face. Karim's voice died away.

"I need you to babysit," Lamia said. "No arguments, please, Karim. I can't leave the girls next door with Rasha's mother because she's gone to a funeral. Anyway, Sireen's earache's bad again and she wants to stay at home. Your father's got to get back to the shop and I've got an appointment in town."

"Why's it got to be me?" Karim said as crossly as he dared, keeping a wary eye on his father. "Can't anyone else? Where's Jamal anyway?"

"Working for his exams with Basim, as you well know, and I

don't want to hear another word out of you," his mother snapped back. "It's about time you started pulling your weight at home. Slipping off all the time, never telling us where you are, coming home filthy. That paint all over you the other day! All over everything! And don't keep telling me you're working on an art project with Joni. What do you take me for? Even when you're here you're always in a dream. I don't know what's gotten into you. Sireen needs her medicine at four o'clock, no later. One teaspoon from the bottle in the fridge. And try to stop Farah from bugging her. The poor little soul needs to be kept quiet."

Karim slunked back to his room and threw himself on his bed. He could hear his mother collecting her things, going in and out of her bedroom, looking for her keys, changing into her outdoor shoes. He heard the front door shut as his father left the apartment, and minutes later his mother looked into his room.

"Don't forget. One teaspoon at four o'clock. From the bottle in the fridge."

Then she was gone.

Karim groaned and sat up. The others would be making for Hopper's ground by now. They'd be wondering where he was. He reached down into his schoolbag for his cell phone, congratulating himself on getting a new card for it at last, then he sent a quick text message off to Joni.

He had just finished when he heard a sound from the next room. Farah's voice was raised in a high whine. She was pretending to imitate Sireen, he knew, teasing her, trying to make her cry.

He went to the door and threw it open.

"Hey, you," he said, glaring at Farah, who was sitting on the sofa beside Sireen and had turned to stare at him, her face alight with speculative mischief. "Outside. You're going downstairs to play with Rasha and the other kids, and you're not coming back up till Mama comes home."

Farah smirked.

"Rasha's not here. She's gone off with her mama."

"Not true. I saw her half an hour ago hanging around downstairs. And even if she isn't there, the other kids are. You've got—" he looked at his watch—"three minutes to leave this apartment, or... "

"Or what?" said Farah, with interest.

"Or I'll lock you in your bedroom and won't let you go out to play with anyone at all," said Karim, inspired.

To his relief, the threat worked. With a scowl and a mutter, Farah retrieved her Barbie from its corner behind the TV, wrapped a grubby shred of blanket around it and carried it towards the door, deliberately leaving it wide open behind her.

Karim shut it and turned to Sireen. She was lying on the sofa, her thumb in her mouth, the corners of which were turned down.

"Want a drink," she said.

He fetched her some juice from the fridge and sat beside her as she drank it. The rest of the afternoon yawned ahead of him. He selected a Tom and Jerry cartoon from the rack of DVDs and put it on, then settled beside her and watched it too.

By the end of the tape, Sireen was asleep. Karim, bored and restless, went into the kitchen and stepped out onto the balcony. Sheets were hanging out to dry. Since the visit to the village, Farah had had nightmares from time to time, and every time the tension increased in the city, she began to wet her bed again.

Karim parted the nearly dry sheets and looked out over the parapet. The roads running between the new apartment buildings that dotted about the hillside were almost empty. Few cars or people were around. From the parking lot below came the high-pitched sound of children's voices. Farah and Rasha were down there somewhere.

He was about to turn and go back inside when he caught sight of Farah sitting by herself on the steps that led up to the entrance of the building. She was clutching her doll tightly against her chest. Another girl was standing in front of her, her hands on her hips, her head on one side, while several other children stood around and watched.

Karim couldn't hear what the girl was saying, but he saw his sister flinch, then lunge forward and shout something. The other children laughed. Karim could see Rasha now, standing awkwardly against the wall a little ways away, watching and chewing her thumb. The four or five other children began to skip about and chant. The words floated up clearly to the balcony, five floors above.

"Farah smells of wee-wee! Farah smells of wee-wee!"

Pity for his sister and rage at her tormentors sent Karim flying out of the apartment and down the stairs before he knew what he was doing. He burst out of the main door of the building with the energy of a charging bull, his eyes blazing.

"You," he said, pointing to the ringleader, "are a little brat with so much dirt under your fingernails you could grow an olive grove out of your hands." His finger swiveled to the next child. "And your hair's like a bird's nest. It's probably full of worms and bird poo."

The children stared back at him, their mouths open.

"As for you," he said to the next one, "you look as if you've been rolling in donkey dung. You're totally disgusting. I can smell you from here."

He was so impressed with his own inventiveness that his anger had ebbed away.

"What about me?" the smallest child said, edging expectantly in front of the others. "What's wrong with me?"

"Snot coming out of your nose, sleepy dust in your eyes, face like Mickey Mouse, no front teeth," Karim said, unable to stop himself from smiling at the child's pleased expression.

Rasha had sidled around from behind the others and was sitting on the step beside Farah, pressed up against her.

"You want to come in now, Farah?" Karim said casually.

Farah looked sideways at Rasha, who shook her head, then at the others, then up at Karim. She swallowed and said, "Walid hasn't really got worms in his hair, Karim. Only caterpillars."

The joke wasn't very funny, but the others laughed, their bullying forgotten.

"Suit yourself," Karim said. He turned to go back up the stairs, catching a smile of dazzling gratitude from Farah as he reached the main door.

He felt satisfied and masterful as he let himself back into the apartment and checked the time, woke Sireen, gave her her medicine and set up another cartoon for her to watch.

He'd been shocked by the sight of Farah, miserably alone, the object of the others' teasing. He'd never really thought about her as a real person. A real child. He'd only ever seen her as a nuisance. Now that he came to think of it, though, she'd been different lately, more easily scared, less assertive, crying at the sound of loud voices, becoming frantic at the sound of explosions or distant gunfire.

He yawned. The last hour of the afternoon stretched endlessly ahead. There was nothing he wanted to do, nothing he could settle on. He could think only of Hopper and Joni, and wonder what they were doing at Hopper's ground.

Joni phoned half an hour after Lamia came home.

"The flag looks even better," he said. "We found more paint and made it bigger. You can see it from miles away now."

"Great," said Karim enviously.

"The paint dripped all over the place though. We got green in our hair and everywhere. 'Specially Hopper. He looks like a Martian. Are you coming tomorrow?"

"Can't. Got to babysit again. The neighbor's still away. Thursday maybe."

"See you, then."

"Yes, see you."

Chapter Eighteen

There's never any time for anything now, Karim kept telling himself. Life had indeed become more stressful. The teachers at school were laying on a heavy load of work, anxious, after the weeks of disruption, to make up for lost time; certain, too, that it would not be long before Israeli tanks rolled back into town to bring the curfew down and lock everyone inside their houses again.

Karim did his best at school, but he couldn't concentrate. His thoughts kept sliding back, as if on oiled wheels, to Hopper's ground. It had assumed wonderful dimensions in his imagination. The soccer area was still central, of course—it would always be the most important thing—but there were little offshoots to it as well now. He mentally constructed a stadium, small but perfect, and a press stand and changing rooms for the players. Then—why not?—at the edge there'd be a whole area, a little street almost, with all the places he liked best. An Internet café where they'd have all the best games and they'd never have to pay and they'd always be first in line. And stalls selling drinks and snacks. And a little cinema, which would only show the most exciting films.

The dream always faded more quickly than it should have. The bubble always burst. An Internet cafe? Was he crazy? A cinema? Snack stalls? There wasn't even room, at Hopper's ground, to play a decent game of soccer. It was just a piece of ground, that was all, with a mass of rubble along one side.

Very often, at this point, Karim's dream coincided with a nasty reminder of present-day reality, a smack on the head from Mr. Mohammed, or a sharp question from another teacher who was suddenly standing over him, shaming him in front of the whole class.

There was no chance to actually go back to Hopper's ground and get on with things. It wasn't only the mounds of homework he was supposed to be doing. Rasha's mother was back and was looking after the girls as usual while Lamia was at work, but his father kept asking him to help out at the shop after school.

Hassan Aboudi had lifted himself out of the depression that had started to paralyze him and was doggedly trying to make a go of his business again, setting up a new window display and poring over catalogues, trying to predict what might possibly tempt the hard-pressed citizens of Ramallah to part with their dwindling supplies of cash. Karim's job was to continue with the endless clearing up, the sweeping and cleaning, and to hold the fort in the front of the shop, in case a customer should come in, while his father saw to things in the storeroom at the back.

In spite of his preoccupations, Karim couldn't help noticing that Jamal was more tense and tight-lipped than usual. The photo of Violette, carefully hidden between books on a high shelf (out of reach of Farah's inquisitively probing fingers) was still taken out and gazed upon at frequent intervals, but Jamal appeared to have other things on his mind as well. The card on his cell phone had run out at last and he was forced to resort to the family's land line. Calls from his best friend, Basim, always frequent, had multiplied. In the past the two of them had usually met down in the town in the evenings, hanging out around the cafés or shopping malls, but Karim sensed that something else was afoot. Jamal was definitely up to something.

It was mid-afternoon on a Wednesday. Karim had been reluctantly helping his father to move boxes from the back to the front of the shop. Released at last, he was leaving to go home when he caught sight of Jamal and Basim walking fast along the other side of the street, weaving through the crowds of people, dodging between the bins that street sellers had set up on every spare corner of pavement. They looked so intent and purposeful, so taut with determination, that Karim's curiosity was aroused.

"I'm going to see Joni, Baba," he called to his father, at the back of the shop. "I won't be home late, I promise."

Then he slipped across the road and, keeping out of sight, began to follow the older boys.

It was difficult at first. The pavements were crowded and Karim was too short to see over people's heads, but it was easier once Jamal and Basim had passed the main shopping area.

Karim had expected them to carry on down the wide road that led out of the old center of Ramallah towards Kalandia, the main checkpoint on the road to Jerusalem, where Israeli troops manned permanent sandbagged gun nests, a high watchtower and a complex system of concrete-wall channels which tightly controlled the flow of traffic, sometimes allowing people to pass and then, without warning, shutting the checkpoint so that turmoil was created on either side. To his surprise, however, they turned suddenly to the right and began to stride down the steep hill, where the road was lined by new apartment blocks. It was harder for Karim to keep out of sight here, in this residential area, where there were few people and no street stalls among which he could hide, but Jamal and Basim were so intent and purposeful, bouncing, almost, on the balls of their feet as they walked, that Karim didn't think they'd be likely to turn round.

They had nearly reached the bottom of the slope, where the steep street ran into another lying along the side of the hill. Karim, still halfway up, heard shouted greetings and saw two other young men run towards them from the left. He screwed up his eyes, trying to recognize them. It was difficult because they had each wrapped a black and white checked keffiyeh around their head and the lower half of their face, leaving only their eyes exposed, but he was fairly sure that the shorter, stockier one was Basim's brother, and the tall, lithe one in the zip-up denim jacket was Tarik, the coolest guy among Jamal's set of friends, the one the others all looked up to.

Tarik and Basim's brother were pointing back towards the way they had come, and all four young men started off in that direction, then almost at once stopped again. Tarik pointed to Jamal's neck, then to Basim's. Karim, who had sneaked down as far as the junction and was peering round at them from the shelter of a high stone wall, saw Jamal and Basim take off their own keffiyehs, which they were wearing in the normal way as scarves around their necks, and wrap them around their heads in imitation of the other two. He was close enough to hear them talk in the quietness of this residential street.

"Have you got a sling?" Tarik asked Jamal.

"No," Jamal answered.

Karim nearly snorted out loud. Jamal? Mr. Butterfingers himself? Throwing stones from a sling? In spite of the tension that was knotting up his stomach, Karim was glad he'd come. Jamal was going to make a total mess of this, he was sure of it. It would be a pleasure to watch.

Tarik reached inside his pocket and handed Jamal a long, thin strip of cloth. Jamal took it and pulled it taut, pretending to test its strength. Tarik looked at Basim, who pulled a sling from his own pocket and dangled it proudly in front of Tarik's eyes. It was made of a small strip of rubber, from the inner tube of a car tire, with pieces of string attached to either end.

"Excellent."

Tarik patted Basim on the shoulder, nodded at Jamal, then set off at the head of the little group. Karim rounded the corner after them and, slipping quickly from one protective gateway to the next, followed as closely as he dared.

Their goal was soon apparent. The empty side road they were on soon ran into a much busier one coming up from the valley below. A flying Israeli roadblock had been set up here. An armored Jeep with a yellow light flashing on the roof blocked one half of the road, and a tank a little further on jutted right out across the other side, so that anyone passing through, on foot or in a car, would have to weave their way past both, under the barrel of the tank's big gun. No one at all was going through at the moment. Barbed wire had been rolled out right across the road and wickedly pointed "dragon's teeth," designed to shred the tires of any cars that ran over them, were scattered across the ground. News of the barricade seemed to have spread, because no one was lining up to cross. Anyone coming this way would have taken in the situation at a glance and turned to find another, much longer, way around.

Karim felt the usual punch of fear and hatred at the sight of the enemy. He could see from the tautness in the four young men in front of him that they were feeling it too. They were collecting stones now as they went, needing only to bend down in order to scoop up any number of small rocks and bits of broken concrete, smashed pieces of pavement, which the tanks had all but pulverized.

Tarik, the leader in every way, had been holding the others back while they settled the stones into the pouches of their slings. Then, with an ear-splitting yell in which Karim could just distinguish the words "Free Palestine!" he ran forward, whirling his long-stringed catapult expertly round his head. He released one string of it with a final flick of the wrist. The stone smacked into the side of the armored Jeep with a satisfying clang and bounced off it down to the ground.

The reaction was as instant as if he'd hit a hornets' nest. Of the five Israeli soldiers, three had been on the far side of the tank, laughing at an old farmer who, with panicky haste, was trying to turn a small truck loaded with vegetables in the narrow confines of the road. Two of them came running at once, while the third climbed hastily into the tank and began to maneuver its gigantic gun barrel to face the boys.

By now, Basim and his brother had fired off their stones too. Basim's had hit the ground just short of the Jeep. His brother's, by a lucky chance, had whistled close past the steel helmet of one of the two soldiers who had been leaning against the Jeep. They instantly retreated behind their vehicle and, using it as a barricade, laid their rifles along the roof of it and took aim at the boys down their sights.

Cold fear ran through Karim's veins, but excitement was possessing him as well. He was watching Jamal, who was fumbling ineptly with his sling. Only a few moments ago, Karim had wanted to see Jamal make a mess of it, but now, with his whole heart, he wanted his brother to do it well, to send off a peach of a missile in a perfect arc, one that would hit a hated soldier between the eyes and lay him out cold.

"Go on, you big idiot," he muttered out loud, as Jamal's sling, in imitation of Tarik's, went twirling in a circle through the air. For a moment, the shot looked good, then, just as Karim knew he would, Jamal let go too soon and the stone, shooting harmlessly off to the side, hit a wall and fell limply to the ground.

The others were keeping up the hail of missiles and issuing bloodcurdling cries.

"Death to Israel!"

"Free Palestine!"

"*Allah u Akbar!*"

Jamal had thrown away his sling in disgust. He was picking up stone after stone and hurling them with his bare hands. Karim felt his fingers curl as if round a stone of his own. His feet twitched with the desire to run forward and join the others. Instead he stood indecisively, more afraid of Tarik and Jamal than of the Israelis.

They'll be furious with me for following them, he told himself. Jamal will go on and on.

The soldiers had been shouting in Hebrew, but now they were ominously quiet. Another of Tarik's stones hit the roof of the Jeep and skidded over to the other side. It acted on the soldiers like a signal. They hunched over their rifles and two shots rang out almost simultaneously.

Karim flinched at the report and ducked away, and he saw that Jamal and Basim had instinctively crouched down too, but Tarik was taking no notice of the deadly danger he was in. His sling was spinning, dervish-like, round his swathed head again, and another stone flew through the air, to land harmlessly, this time, against the heavy wire mesh that covered the Jeep's windscreen. The soldiers' bullets, too, had gone wide.

Then, from behind, Karim heard the sound he'd been unconsciously expecting: the whine of sirens. The man in the tank must have been calling up reinforcements. They'd be cornered now, if they weren't careful. They'd end up with broken arms and legs, and cracked skulls too, if they were unlucky, in an Israeli prison.

"Jamal! Basim! They're coming! Quick! From behind!" he screamed, breaking cover and racing towards his brother. "You've got to run! Now!"

Jamal was in the act of picking up another stone. Karim could see only his eyes between the folds of the keffiyeh. They'd been hot and red with anger, but caution leapt into them now.

Pushing Karim aside, he shouted, "Basim! Come on! They're coming! Tarik! Both of you!"

Karim had expected them to run back the way they'd come, but further shots from behind the Jeep were forcing them to take instant cover. Following Tarik, they vaulted lightly over a wall into the grounds of an apartment complex and, dashing through the underground parking garage, came up the other side.

It was a wild scramble back up the hill. They dodged around the sides of buildings, in and out of doors and gates, swarmed up the crumbling walls of the ancient terraces, darted across roads and through the stone-strewn remnants of old olive groves, until at last they reached the crowded streets above and knew that they were safe.

It was in the last rush up a back street that the accident happened. Jamal, busy peeling the keffiyeh off his head, was blinded for a moment by its folds and crashed into the corner of an air conditioner that was protruding out of a window over the pavement. The sharp edge of it caught him on the temple and blood began to trickle down his face.

Karim, as anxious as the others to put the greatest possible distance between himself and the soldiers' bullets, had also been keeping his distance from Jamal, but when he saw Jamal hit the air conditioner and stagger backwards, and the bright blood glistening on his brother's forehead, he ran up to him.

"Are you OK?"

Jamal shot him a furious look.

"Of course I am. What do you think? Bashing my head open and nearly knocking myself out's my favorite activity."

Under the red flow his face had gone pale. He shut his eyes as if he felt faint. Karim nudged up against him, to support him, and Jamal unwillingly put his hand on Karim's shoulder to steady himself.

"Were you down there for long?" Karim said artlessly. "Did you get any hits in? I heard them shooting. Were they rubber bullets or live rounds?"

Jamal opened his eyes and looked down at him suspiciously.

Karim fished in his pocket, found a dusty crumpled tissue and handed it to Jamal, who held it under the wound to stop the blood from flowing into his eyes.

"You know perfectly well how long we were there. You followed us, you little creep," he said.

Karim assumed an expression of injured innocence.

"Followed you? Would I bother? I was up by Uncle Mohammed's place, and I heard shouting and went down to have a look."

The cut on Jamal's head, though not deep, was still gushing blood. He dabbed at it with the end of his keffiyeh and succeeded only in smearing blood across his forehead. Basim, who had reached the main road above, came hurrying back down.

"Jamal! What happened? Hey, did they get you? Are you OK?"

"It's nothing," said Jamal. "I just—"

Before he could say any more, there was a shriek from further up the hill. Looking up, the boys saw a crowd of girls staring at them with horror on their faces. In the middle of them was Violette. She ran down ahead of the others, and a minute later they were all hovering admiringly around Jamal like a crowd of agitated butterflies.

"We saw your brother up there," one of them said to Basim. "He told us there'd been a clash. We heard them shooting. He didn't say anyone was hit though. My God, they must have been shooting live rounds! How deep is it?"

Violette twitched the keffiyeh out of Jamal's nerveless fingers, took off her own flowered scarf and began to gently dab at Jamal's forehead with it. Jamal had shut his eyes again, but the pallor of his cheeks had turned to a healthy red blush.

"A half inch lower and it would have entered the brain," Violette said earnestly, eliciting murmurs of outrage from the other girls. "You would have been a martyr."

Jamal looked sideways at Karim, who rolled his eyes derisively.

"Do you feel faint? Shouldn't you get this looked at in the hospital?" Violette's voice throbbed with compassion.

Jamal squared his shoulders bravely.

"It's fine. It's OK. Just a scratch, that's all."

"But the shock! The loss of blood!"

Revolted, Karim cleared his throat.

Jamal grabbed his arm above the elbow and squeezed it in a painful but trembling grip.

"I really am fine. You're so...so sweet to... "

Karim, his stomach turning, tried to pull away. Jamal's grip tightened.

"We've got to go," Jamal said reluctantly. "There'll be a fuss at home if we're late."

"My God, yes. They'll be frantic when they see you've been shot," said Violette.

"Oh, I won't tell them." Jamal looked noble. "I'll say I hit my head on an air conditioner or something."

Karim choked. Violette didn't notice. She was brushing Jamal's forehead one last time with her scarf.

"It's hardly bleeding now. Look after him, Karim. Make him sit down if he feels faint or anything."

Karim was already dragging Jamal away.

"You...you... " Karim began, when they were out of earshot.

Jamal, in a happy dream, didn't seem to have heard him.

"Jamal, you con artist. You total, total creep."

Jamal looked down at him.

"Did you see her? Did you see how she looked at me? She actually mopped up my blood with her very own scarf! My blood! What? What are you looking at me like that for?"

"You're disgusting. Letting her think you'd been shot."

Jamal grinned.

"What could I do? I didn't say it myself. She just assumed it. I didn't tell a lie."

"No, but you...I mean... " Words failed Karim.

Jamal suddenly frowned.

"You were about to tell, weren't you?"

"I wasn't! Who do you think I am?"

"Yes, you were. I saw."

"I didn't tell though, did I? And I'm not going to, either, so you can get off my back."

He wriggled his shoulders defensively.

"You'd better not if you know what's good for you. No one. Not even Joni." Jamal's hand was sliding into his inner pocket. "Otherwise I'll take this back again and sell it to someone else."

He put a small, square, flat box into Karim's hand.

"Lineman!" Karim's face lit up. "How did you get the money? Did you sell your guitar?"

Jamal looked embarrassed.

"No. If you must know, I took the necklace back to the shop."

Karim was touched at this sacrifice.

"Oh, well," he said consolingly. "It didn't look like you needed it just then. She was totally impressed. You were doing great. I could tell."

Jamal rearranged the keffiyeh around his neck so that the bloodstains were more visible. He was clearly enjoying the curious and sympathetic glances of the passers-by.

"Actually, I would have taken it back anyway. Basim told me he's been talking to his cousin and she said that kind of jewelry's totally out of fashion. Looks like I got it wrong."

Karim tucked the little plastic box securely into his own pocket.

"I see," he said, though he was still befogged by the convoluted workings of his brother's mind. "Just don't take it away again, OK? I need this game. I need it. If anything happens to it, you know what I'll do?"

"I get the message. No need to spell it out." Jamal draped an affectionate arm around Karim's shoulders and together they walked home.

Chapter Nineteen

News of the latest clash with the Israelis, and of Jamal's heroic wound, spread as fast as a bush fire through the youth of Ramallah, and for several days, while the dressing covering the wound on his forehead was still visible to all, Jamal was treated like a hero. Everyone admired his self-deprecating modesty. His ironic insistence, to all but a chosen few, that he hadn't really been shot at all, was greeted with nods, winks and murmurs of, "He's only trying to spare his mother the anxiety."

Karim, though he rejoiced in the return of Lineman, had no time in which to play it. It seemed to him that he was busier than he had ever been in his whole life, running between school, the shop and clandestine meetings with his friends. In his better moments, he could conjure up the ideal vision of Hopper's ground in his mind. In his worst moments, he could see only a dusty, uneven vacant lot and a sense of futility would depress him.

There was a pattern now to the boys' meetings. They normally reached Hopper's ground at more or less the same time in the middle of the afternoon. By then, Joni had finished school, Karim, after his own, earlier school hours, had done a stint at the shop and Hopper had finished most of the chores his mother had given him. He seemed to have given up on trying to sell Koranic verses in the town. It made so little money it wasn't worth doing.

As soon as everyone arrived, they'd dive straight into the car and check up on the cats (Joni never forgot to bring food for them, and Karim sometimes managed a bit as well). They'd fetch out their hidden clothes and change, kick the ball around for a while, then get started on the next task they'd set themselves.

"If we could just get that huge rock out of the way," Karim said to the other two, as they rested, panting, after a particularly energetic game.

"That thing? Are you kidding?" Joni picked up a pebble and threw it at the big rock, which was disastrously positioned near the very centre of the playing area. The pebble pinged against it and bounced off mockingly. "We can't possibly move it. We're stuck with it."

He got up and disappeared into the car, returning a moment later with a bottle of orange soda, one of the small stock he'd been amassing since Karim had suggested the idea. He held out the fizzing bottle to his friends and they drank from it in turn.

Hopper wiped his mouth, went up to the rock, leaned against it and pushed at it with all his strength. Wordlessly, he gave up and came back to Joni, holding his hand out for the bottle.

Karim frowned. The others' defeatism annoyed him. He looked at the rock, his eyes narrowed. People did move big things. The ancient Egyptians had done it. Brute force wasn't enough. You had to be clever—to work things out.

He went over to the rock and circled around it, studying it. It was embedded in the hard-baked soil. He kicked at the ground at its base. A little fountain of dust puffed up. The earth wasn't packed too tightly there.

The chilling wail of a siren sounded out above the still, cool city. Instinctively, all three boys flinched and looked around.

"It's one of ours. An ambulance," Joni said uncertainly.

They waited for a moment, listening for anything else, for shouts or shots, the explosion of a tank shell or the sound of heavy engines. The siren sounded again, more distant this time. Whatever the action was, it was moving away.

Without comment, Karim resumed his study of the rock. Then he trotted over to the rubble pile, selected a sharp broken tile and returned to the rock with it. He bent down and began to hack at the earth around the base. It was breaking up more easily than he had expected. He scooped the loose earth away with his hands.

The others had wandered off.

"No, you're standing all wrong," Joni was saying. "Karate's an art. You have to put your feet like this, and balance...."

Karim, intent on his task, stopped listening to them.

He'd moved quite a lot of earth away now. He stood up, choosing the right place carefully, put his hands against the rock and pushed. He felt a tiny movement.

"Hey, you two! It's moving! Come and help!" he called out.

Joni and Hopper joined him. They leaned against the rock and braced themselves, then, holding their breath, they heaved.

There was another minute shift.

"Come on! Again!" panted Karim.

They tried again. Karim felt the blood rush to his head with the effort, and the sinews of his shoulders strain and tremble. They sensed another momentary wobble, then the rock was still again.

"It's no good," Joni said, straightening up and dusting off his hands.

"It is. We've got to do it," insisted Karim.

Hopper was looking out towards the road. The late session had just ended at the school in the refugee camp and seven or eight boys were walking past.

"I know them," Hopper said. He raised his voice. "Hey, Mahmoud! Ali! You guys! Over here!"

The boys sauntered over.

"Who made this flag? It's awesome," one of them said.

"We did," Hopper, Karim and Joni replied together.

"What are you doing now?" one of the new boys asked.

"Moving this rock."

"What for?"

"We're making a soccer field. The rock's in the way."

The boy grinned.

"Cool idea."

He dropped his bag and put his shoulder to the stone. The others joined him as best they could, jostling for space to push.

Karim, elbowed aside by a tall boy with massive shoulders, stepped back, biting his lip. He wasn't sure about this. Hopper's ground was their place, his and Joni's and Hopper's. He didn't know these boys. They weren't his friends. He didn't want strangers taking over.

Then he saw that the stone was beginning to give way. It was tilting, tipping, rocking on its base.

"Yes!" he shouted. "*Wahid! Thnen! Telatte!* One! Two! Three! He-e-ave!"

Out of the corner of his eye he saw that someone passing down the road had halted at the sound of his voice and turned around, but he was too excited to take more notice.

"It's going!" he yelled. "One more push!"

The rock, moving as unwillingly as a tree wrenched bodily from its roots, rolled out of its resting place and rocked to a standstill. The man in the road was approaching now. Karim ignored him.

"Keep it going!" he called out, dancing up and down on the spot. "Keep pushing! Right over out of the way. Roll it! More! More! Yes!"

Good-naturedly, the boys obeyed.

With a satisfying rumble, and much more easily than he would have thought possible, the rock rolled right across the dry baked ground and came at last to a stop beside the wall of rubble.

"Karim?" said a familiar voice. "What on earth are you doing?"

Karim turned to see Jamal staring down at him.

"Making a soccer field," he said, too flushed with triumph to care that his long-held secret had been discovered. "You should have seen this place when we started. We've moved loads and loads of rubbish. It's going to be great now. And we made the flag."

"*You* did all this? You kids?"

"Yes. Me and Joni and Hopper. That's Hopper, over there."

Jamal's eyes widened with unwilling respect.

"Well, well. I have to say that I'm impressed. So this is what you've been up to all this time."

"Yes, and you've no idea how much work it's been. See all those stones over there? We...."

Jamal shook his head.

"Tell me later. Listen, you've got to get home now. Haven't you heard the news? There's been another bombing operation. The Israelis—"

"Anyone got a ball?" one of the new boys was calling out.

Karim, alert to the sharp note in Jamal's voice, was nevertheless drawn irresistibly to the lure of a possible game.

"Yes, it's somewhere over there," he called out over his shoulder, pointing vaguely towards the place where they'd stopped playing, then he looked back at Jamal, checking his face for signs of real urgency.

Jamal shrugged.

"You've got half an hour, I suppose. The Israelis are bringing the curfew down again, everyone says. The tanks are coming back in. It'll take them a bit of time to get here though. Listen out for them and don't take risks. I'll have Mama on my back forever more if you get caught outside in the curfew."

Karim nodded.

"Did you hear that?" he called to the others. "The tanks are coming back in."

"Not yet, though," one of the boys said. "They never come till after six. Where's that ball?"

"Here," said Joni, retrieving the ball from the dip it had rolled into.

"Look, there's even a goal up there," a boy called Latif said, pointing to the wall at the far end of the ground where, a week earlier, Karim had painstakingly outlined the shape of a goalmouth with a black marker pen against the rough stones.

Seconds later, a couple of schoolbags, roughly positioned, had created another goal at the opposite end, the boys had sorted themselves into two teams and a furious game was in progress. Karim darted in between Hopper and one of the new boys, and, taking the ball in a superb tackle, began to dribble it down the field.

"Karim!" he heard Jamal call. "Don't stay too long. Half an hour, no more. I can't wait for you. I've got to see Basim."

Then everything else was wiped from his mind as the game took over.

One of the new boys began to mark him, trying, with neat stabs of his feet, to get the ball away from him. He was good. The challenge was real. Karim felt his inner self rise up to meet it. His focus narrowed. He was willing the ball to stay with him, aware of a new deftness in his feet as he feinted and dodged, touching the ball now with delicate coaxing strokes from the side of a foot, now punching at it with masterful short kicks from the toes.

The home stretch was suddenly in front of him, the last run down to the wall and the lines of the goalmouth. The boy guarding it was half crouching, his arms held out, but Karim could read his mind. As the boy jumped to the right, he aimed for the left. Perfectly timed, perfectly judged, his foot sliced the ball up into a magnificent arc and it bounced against the wall just inside the corner of the post and crossbar.

At once the game moved on. Karim's worthy opponent was running the ball fast down to the far end, with Hopper and Joni in pursuit, but for a second or two Karim couldn't move. The moment was too beautiful. His feelings threatened to choke him.

They'd achieved something real, the three of them, at Hopper's ground. They'd made a good place out of a rubbish heap. There would never be a stadium as there was in his dreams, no spectators, no TV cameras or scribbling reporters, but all of those things could wait. The important thing was the place, this space that was their own creation.

Today, something new had happened. These other boys—it was great, after all, that they had come. There could be real soccer games, with teams, now. And then there was Jamal. He'd approved of everything. He'd admired them. Karim felt that the two halves of his life, painfully divided, might after all come together.

But best of all, more important than anything else, was the soccer, the marvelous harmony he could feel between his brain, his eyes and his feet, the magic in his every move, the power and skill coursing through him.

He was about to launch himself joyfully back into the game when he heard, much too close, the sound of heavy vehicles—tanks, or bulldozers or both—rumbling up the road. "Watch out! They're coming! They're here!" he yelled at the top of his voice.

"*Mamnou'a al tajwwol!*" a loudspeaker suddenly blared out. "Being outside is forbidden!"

Chapter Twenty

The sound and sight of the three huge Israeli tanks sent the blood pounding through Karim. His senses sharpened and every hair stood on end.

The other boys were scattering, leaping up and over the rubble to disappear on the far side.

"Come on!" Joni was calling. "Be quick!"

Karim turned to shout goodbye to Hopper, and was about to run after Joni when he stopped, aghast. Instead of fleeing across the rubble, like the other boys, Hopper was running straight for the leading tank.

"Hopper!" Karim yelled. "Stop! Are you crazy?"

Then he saw, on the far side of the road, an old man who had been pushing a wheelbarrow heaped with vegetables. In his haste to get out of the way of the tanks, he'd upset his load, and now he was scrabbling around, trying to gather up a few of the tomatoes, eggplants and peppers which were rolling down the gutter.

He straightened up, and Karim saw that it was Hopper's grandfather.

"Leave them, *sidi*! Go inside!" he heard Hopper shout.

The old man hesitated, and then the foremost tank began to slow and the huge gun barrel swung around towards him.

The old man began to run awkwardly away, the long skirt of his robe flapping around his legs.

Karim took off himself, flying towards the rubble, then up the side and over it, his back crawling at the thought that the soldiers' rifles might be trained on him.

He looked back one last time but, taking his eyes off his feet, trod on a loose cinder block which rolled under his weight, tipping him over. He felt a sharp, agonizing pain in his ankle and fell awkwardly, wrenching it even more badly.

He tried to get up and crawl on. There were shouts now, coming from the tanks, but he couldn't make out the Hebrew words. He slipped again and rolled into a dip, badly grazing the ball of his right hand.

The tanks had halted.

They've seen me. They're coming to get me, he thought, his throat tight with panic.

He looked over his shoulder. The dip he was in was deeper than he'd realized. He was out of sight of the tanks and crews. He could see nothing but sky and the peaks of rubble all around. But the shouts were more urgent than ever.

Very cautiously, ignoring his bleeding right hand, he sat up and peered out through a crack between two rusting oil drums.

Hopper was down there alone, one wild, slim, impish figure. He was dancing about in front of the first tank, a creature possessed, moving like quicksilver, the very spirit of resistance. As Karim watched, he bent and scooped something up from the ground in a movement so subtle and fluid it was barely visible. Karim narrowed his eyes. What was that in his hand? He could make out a glint of shiny purple.

"An eggplant!" he muttered under his breath. "What on earth does he want an eggplant for?"

Hopper was holding the eggplant with ostentatious caution. Defiantly, he raised it to his mouth and bit off the green stem. It looked exactly as if he was tearing the pin out of a hand grenade. Then he aimed the eggplant and hurled it at the tank.

The man on the tank turret, a grey-yellow figure muffled in

body armor topped off with a steel helmet, had been following the mercurial, dancing boy down the sights of his M16 rifle, trying in vain to get a fix on him. He shouted a warning and ducked as the eggplant flew towards him. It splattered squashily against the side of the tank.

Karim's fists were balled with tension but his heart was on fire with admiration.

"Awesome, Hopper, incredible!" he mouthed silently. "But run now. Run!"

Instead of running away, Hopper again raced directly towards the tank. As Karim watched, his heart standing still, Hopper leapt for the massive gun barrel. For what seemed like an endless moment, he swung from it, as casually as if it was a bar in a playground.

It had seemed to Karim, watching from the rubble pile, as if Hopper was wrapped round in a bright sheath of glory, impregnable, unconquerable, but it was surely impossible now that his luck would hold. Soldiers were popping up like rabbits from the turrets of the tanks behind. They were shouting at each other and aiming their rifles.

Karim couldn't bear to watch. He squeezed his eyes tightly shut and smacked his uninjured fist against his forehead. Shots rang out and there were more shouts. Karim imagined Hopper's lifeless body crumpled on the pavement. He had to look.

What he saw was his friend's lithe figure dodging and diving, leaping erratically down the side street that led to the impenetrable lanes of the refugee camp. Shots were flying after him, shattering stones, embedding themselves in walls. Hopper flinched once, slapping his left hand to his right elbow, and then he was gone, out of sight, safe in the camp's tight embrace.

Karim, trembling and sweating, breathed out a great gust of relief. Some of the crews from different tanks were conferring together, huddled behind a huge bulldozer. Then they ran back to their own vehicles and began to turn them to face the camp, so that their huge gun barrels were pointing directly down into the densely packed buildings.

They're going to go in there and shoot it all up and knock down buildings till they find him, Karim thought.

The elation that had thrilled him while he was watching Hopper's great defiance had gone. Now he felt only weak and ashamed. Why hadn't he been there, standing up for Palestine, holding up an armored column all on his own, armed with nothing but an eggplant? Why hadn't he had the courage to insult the Israelis by swinging insolently on their very own gun barrel? Why was he lying here, while they were about to go on down, bent on a murderous, destructive rampage?

Then, unexpectedly, the tanks moved again, turning away from the camp, facing back up towards the town.

They're going to move on after all, Karim told himself, with a shudder of relief.

He'd wait until they were well up the road and everything was quiet, then he'd creep down off the rubble and limp home, as quickly as his sprained ankle would let him, slipping through the back streets that the Israelis hadn't yet had time to occupy.

He gathered himself, ready to make his move, but although the tanks were revving up, their engines deafeningly loud in the now deserted street, they were not yet moving on.

Karim cautiously raised his head a little higher, trying to see, then ducked down again. The soldiers had noticed the Palestinian flag made of stones laid out at the entrance to Hopper's ground. Two of them were kicking at it with their boots, breaking it up, swearing at it, if the tone of their voices was anything to go by.

Karim clenched his fists, feeling even more helpless and humiliated.

"Get out! Get out!" he muttered. "This is our place. Get out of here."

163

But the soldiers were looking further ahead into Hopper's ground. Now they were calling over their shoulders to the column of tanks. The man on the foremost turret stood up, his rifle held ready in the firing position. He was high up now, on a level with the top of the rubble. He could see right across it. Only a sheet of corrugated iron, miraculously placed at the edge of the dip where Karim had fallen, was shielding Karim from view.

Karim lay as close to the stones as he could, his face pressed down, willing the man not to see him, willing himself to be invisible.

The seconds crept by. Then he heard more shouts and the engines roared as the tanks began to move. He could hear them rumbling past up the road and he breathed again, waiting for the sound to die away. It didn't. Some vehicles had gone, but some were still near, and coming nearer still.

With a chill of horror that set his whole body shaking, Karim realized that the last of the tanks was rolling right into Hopper's ground.

Chapter Twenty-One

Karim lay in the rubble, moving as little as possible, straining to hear what was happening. They'll go in a minute, he kept telling himself. They'll go on into town.

He could tell that the huge machine was still there, turning, churning the ground, its engines revving. He could hear stones clattering down, and grinding sounds, as if metal was being crushed.

Very cautiously, he edged along the dip behind the sheet of rusting corrugated iron, looking for a suitable peephole. He found a good one. He could watch from here and still be out of sight.

Two vehicles were now in Hopper's ground, a tank and an armored Jeep. Thick wire mesh covered the Jeep's side windows and windshield, and a radio mast, attached to one side, pointed like a long slender lance up into the sky. On its roof was a flashing yellow lamp.

The tank had moved right up onto the soccer field and was turning, not taking any account of the damage it was causing as it did so. Its massive tracks had crashed into the oil drums that had hidden the way into the car and squashed them flat. At the same time it had dislodged a huge pile of stones, which had come tumbling down, making a whole new ridge, so that the car had almost disappeared and was inside the rubble. There was no way into it now from Hopper's ground.

Karim was tempted to make a break for it, to try to crawl away over the rubble to the small side road at the back of Hopper's ground. The soldiers would be unlikely to notice the noise he was sure to make over the roar of the tank's engine. The light was fading, too, as evening approached. Twilight was the best time to move about unnoticed, when everything was grey and dim, and the lights had not yet come on.

He crawled to the far end of the dip and began to climb up the other side, as silently as possible. The tank was still moving. He could see that it was positioning itself at the entrance to Hopper's ground with the gun barrel facing out, towards the refugee camp. The armored Jeep was parked beside it, the yellow light on its roof still flashing. Its occupants had climbed out and were clustering round the tank, talking to the soldier who was perched on the sandbags at the top.

If that guy looks this way, he'll see me, thought Karim.

Fear paralysed him for a moment, but then the man on the turret disappeared down the hatch into the tank. Seizing his chance, Karim scrambled to the top of the rubble peak and slid down the far side.

He found himself lying in another dip, on a flat surface, and realized that by pure chance he had landed on the roof of the car. The shutter that he and Hopper had used to cover the gap in front of the windshield was still in place. Over the last few weeks, bits of old plastic and waste paper had blown on top of it, more or less covering the car's roof too. It was hard to tell, now, that a complete car lay buried under all the rubbish.

Finding it, being right there on top of his own secret place, gave Karim some welcome encouragement. He knew, even in the gathering darkness, exactly where he was, exactly how many ridges of rubble there were still to cross before he reached the edge of Hopper's ground, and which direction he should go in.

He stepped cautiously across the car's roof, ready to move up the next shallow ridge, but just as he had put his foot on the first tumbled mass of rough broken concrete, the tank's engine was switched off and there was silence.

For a moment, he could hear only the rasp of his own breathing and the faint scratch of his shoe on the concrete. But then came the voices of the soldiers, horribly, frighteningly close.

He crouched on top of the car roof and waited. They'd switch the engine of one of the vehicles on again in a minute. There'd be enough noise to cover his escape. They *had* to do it. He *had* to get away.

A moment later, the hoped-for sound came. The Jeep's engine started up. Now it was roaring out of Hopper's ground on screaming tires and careering around the corner.

Karim gathered himself to go on, but before he could move, the Jeep had already stopped. It was now on the far side of the rubble, exactly where Karim would need to go if he was to escape. It was being parked, with noisy changes of gear, in the side road. Its yellow light cast a lurid glow with each flash. On and off. On and off.

I'm trapped, thought Karim. I'm stuck. What if they stay here all night? What if they're here right through the curfew? It could go on for weeks!

The Jeep's engine was still running but the doors had opened and he could hear voices speaking in Hebrew.

They'll search the whole area! Karim told himself. They're certain to! They'll find me hiding, then they'll either shoot me straight off, or beat me up and break my legs, or take me off to prison.

He looked around from side to side, desperate. There was no way out. He had no choice but to stay, and hide.

Moving as quickly as possible, and horribly aware of the noise he was making, which even the sound of the Jeep's engine could hardly cover, Karim slid the old shutter back, slipped under it onto the car's hood beneath and pulled the rough wooden board back over his head. He was hidden now at least, in his own small space.

But I can't stay here, he thought. There's no room. I can't even sit up.

The door to the driver's seat had been ripped off long ago, when the car had been abandoned. The gap it had left made the entrance, which the boys had always used. The tank, though, had pushed the mountain of rubble further in towards it. There was only a narrow crack now between the side of the car, and the mass of broken cinder blocks, stones and smashed concrete.

As quickly as he could, sure that at any moment the Jeep's engine might be switched off and his movements easily heard, Karim eased himself around the side of the car, squeezing himself into the narrow space, catching his clothes on jagged corners, tearing more skin off his hands. Rubble shifted and settled noisily around him. He paused once or twice, and every muscle stiffened, but he heard no angry shouts.

With one last desperate wriggle, he forced his way in and collapsed at last onto the driver's seat. He was filthy, scratched, bruised, exhausted and very, very frightened. But a bit of him was exultant too.

They haven't caught me, he told himself, and they're not going to. I'll be safe in here and I'll stick it out for as long as it takes.

Chapter Twenty-Two

I t was almost completely dark in the car. The last glow of daylight was rapidly fading and only the faint ghostly flashes of the Jeep's yellow emergency light penetrated the gloom.

Karim eased himself through the gap between the front seats into the back of the car. His spare clothes were here and some of Joni's too. He'd need them later, if he had to stay on for a while and the evening chill took hold. His foot dislodged something that slurped as it tilted. Joni's drinks! There were several giant-sized bottles of orange soda left. He felt them with his hands. Four. Four two-liter bottles. He wouldn't be thirsty for a while yet.

He tried to remember if Joni had stored any food here and decided regretfully that he hadn't. It was too dark to look now, anyway.

The Jeep's engine was suddenly switched off and Karim froze, listening to the silence. Then he heard, just beside him, a tiny meow and felt something soft against his hand. It was Ginger, the biggest of the kittens.

Karim picked up the furry ball and held it against his cheek.

"Where's your mama?" he whispered. "Where's Aziza?"

The other kitten laid a tentative paw on his knee. He picked her up with the other hand.

"She'll be back soon," he murmured. "Don't worry."

But he knew his words were empty. How would Aziza find her way back to the car now that the entrance was blocked with a couple of tons of stones and earth? And how would he be able to keep the kittens alive when he didn't have anything but orange soda to give them?

Ginger seemed to read his mind. He extended his claws and drew them down Karim's face, too gently to hurt, but sharp enough to feel.

"Hey, none of that." Karim pulled the kitten away. "We're in this together."

He set Ginger down beside him on the seat and turned the smaller kitten over, so that she lay on her back in his cupped hands, the pale fur of her belly gleaming in the faint light.

We never gave you a name, he thought.

He could feel the metal sides of the car pressing in around him like the walls of a prison and had the odd sensation that they were closing in on him. The kitten in his hands had turned her head and was pressing her nose against his thumb.

Hurriyah, he thought. Freedom. That's what I'll call you. *Hurriyah.*

The presence of the kittens comforted him. They seemed happily unaware of the sounds penetrating the car from outside. Hurriyah, impatient at being held, was trying to wriggle out of Karim's grasp. He set her down beside her brother.

He could hear shouting and running feet. There were metallic sounds, too, as if something was banging against the side of the tank, and from beyond the rubble in the other direction came the noise of the Jeep's doors opening and closing.

They'll have to sleep sometime, Karim thought. I'll wait till it's totally quiet and then try to get away.

But now that he was here, cocooned in this familiar place, the idea of exposing himself to the soldiers' bullets set his heart thumping uncomfortably again. And what would happen if he tried to squeeze back out through the gap and brought earth and rubble tumbling down around him? He could be buried alive! He could be trapped. Suffocated.

Only it won't happen. That's just silly, he told himself sternly. The rubble's not high enough for that.

He felt around on the back seat for his clothes. Here were the clothes he wore to school, the dark trousers, white shirt and woolen sweater. There wasn't much warmth in them, but they'd help a bit when it got really cold.

He shivered, feeling chilled already, and ran his hand further along the seat. Joni's clothes seemed to have gone. No, here they were, folded neatly and piled in the corner. Typical. He almost wanted to smile. He pulled the pile apart. There were more trousers, another long-sleeved shirt and a bomber jacket too. He wouldn't be warm, but he wouldn't freeze to death, even in the middle of the night.

The night! The thought sent his spirits plunging. What would they be thinking at home? Mama would be out of her mind with worry already, crying and carrying on, and Baba—yes, Baba would take it out in anger, ripping up at Jamal for leaving him behind, storing up his fury, probably, to vent on Karim when at last he got home.

He could see his family now, in the kitchen. They'd be sitting down to supper. Mama would have called them to the table. She'd have laid a place for him, expecting him to come dashing in at any moment. She'd have been on the phone for the last hour, calling everyone she knew in case they'd had news of him.

The thought of his empty chair, and the family sitting there without him, brought a rush of tears to his eyes. He might never manage to get home again! Either he'd starve to death here, if the curfew went on for weeks and weeks, or the Israelis would find him, assume he was a terrorist and shoot him.

He wanted to put his face in his hands and sob, but he swallowed his tears, afraid of making a noise.

From far away came the sound of a shot, then another, and a rapid burst of several in a row. There were shouts from the soldiers nearby and the sound of running feet.

Karim lifted his head, turning it as he tried to make out from which direction the sound was coming.

It must be Palestinians shooting, he decided. The soldiers wouldn't be hopping around like fleas if the firing was coming from their side.

A savage joy came, in spite of all his misery. Someone out there was resisting the invaders. And now that he thought about it, he was resisting too, in a way. Just being here, holding out on his own under their very noses, was an act of resistance. Just clinging on, not letting them drive him out of Hopper's ground, was standing up for Palestine.

He held his watch up to the glimmer of light coming through the crack by the driver's seat and his heart sank again. It was only seven thirty! He'd been here barely an hour!

All through the rest of the long, long evening, Karim's spirits rose and fell. The time passed with extraordinary slowness, minutes ticking sluggishly by, quarter hours extending to the length of hours. Hungry, lonely and cold, he shifted around on the back seat, now sitting up, now trying to lie down, unable to stand or stretch right out, trying not to think about his family and the supper they had eaten, trying to devise mind games to pass the time.

Outside, there were occasional shouts, or the wailing of distant sirens, and, once or twice, more bursts of firing, but in between a heavy, sullen silence lay over the occupied city, the inhabitants pinned down in their homes seething with almost audible resentment.

At around nine o'clock a new problem struck. Karim needed to pee. He hated the idea of fouling the inside of the car and having to live with the smell, which might even give him away if a soldier came looking across the rubble. He wriggled about for a bit, thinking out a solution, and then one came. The soda bottle from which he'd drunk was nearly empty. He'd finish the drink off and use that.

He drained the last of the sweet, fizzy liquid and managed quite well to pee into the empty bottle. Then he screwed the cap on tight and hid it under the front passenger seat.

His cleverness cheered him. He lay down again on the back seat, wrapping the spare clothes around him as best he could. The kittens had scrambled into the front of the car, disturbed by his restlessness, and were curled up together on the driver's seat, asleep. So far, hunger and thirst didn't seem to be bothering them.

Karim shut his eyes, willing sleep to come to him too. It didn't. Every time he managed to quiet his mind, a sound from outside made him start, sparking his anxiety again. The cold was attacking him too, and the extra clothes kept slipping off. The car seat was too short and his legs were cramped, while without a pillow his neck was stiffening.

He tossed and turned, hugging himself to keep in the warmth.

He had finally found a comfortable place and was on the verge of sleep when a rattle of loose stones on the roof of the car jerked him awake. He laid still, his heart thudding with fright, then he heard a patter of paws and saw the dark outline of a cat leaping deftly in through the crack by the driver's seat.

"Aziza!" he said softly.

She dropped something she'd been carrying in her mouth onto the front seat beside her kittens, who began to eat, crunching and tearing at the invisible offering, then, ignoring them, she slipped through to the back seat and sniffed at Karim's proffered hand.

With a purr of pleasure, she licked it, rasping it with her rough tongue, then leapt lightly up and settled herself in the crook of his arm.

He felt the warmth of her furry body spreading though him and love, pure love, expanded his heart. Gently he moved his head, as her twitching ear tickled his nose, threatening to make him sneeze.

Quite suddenly, he was asleep.

Chapter Twenty-Three

When Karim woke up to the sound of laughter, he lay for a moment with his eyes closed, wondering what had happened to his pillow, and why his bed had become so hard and narrow, then everything came back to him, and he sat up with a jerk. The movement cricked his stiff neck and jarred his twisted ankle. He moved his foot tentatively from side to side. The ankle still hurt, but it was better than yesterday. He hadn't sprained it badly.

Aziza had gone. The kittens, awake and lively, were tussling with each other on the driver's seat, rolling and clawing, their little teeth bared.

Karim rubbed his stiff, sore neck and looked at his watch. Eight o'clock! He'd slept for hours and hours.

The day stretched ahead, impossibly long and empty. What was he going to do? How would he fill the hours? How could he possibly stay cooped up in this cramped space, still and silent all day long? How would he manage without any food?

He tried not to think about his family and the anxiety they must be enduring, but he couldn't help imagining the breakfast they'd be having, the eggs and bread, the hot tea and creamy yogurt. Saliva rushed into his mouth.

Maybe Joni did leave some food in here, he thought. Some sweets or something. I haven't really looked yet.

He searched carefully through the whole car, pausing for a

heart-stopping moment when he accidentally kicked against a door, which sent out what seemed, to his sensitive ears, to be a deafening clang.

He found nothing. Not a crumb. Not even the peelings of an orange.

He looked at his watch again. Ten past eight. Only ten minutes gone and the whole day to fill.

I'll try and go back to sleep, he thought, lying down again, but he was too wide awake now, and his limbs were twitchy with the need to move.

The laughter that had woken him had stopped, but the voices hadn't gone away. The soldiers were talking in a normal, jokey way. He could pick a few words out from the rapid Hebrew: Ramallah, Jerusalem, terrorist.

The voices stopped, and he heard the unmistakable sound of a ball being kicked, then a scuffing noise as it bounced on the dusty ground, and a sharper bang as it hit the wall.

A red tide rose in his head.

They've found my ball! They're playing with my ball on my field!

Helplessly, he banged his fists down on his knees, hurting himself. This was the worst of all, the last insult, and all he could do was grind his teeth and curse under his breath.

Someone shouted and the soccer game came to an abrupt end. A vehicle was approaching. It stopped moving, but the engine was still running. It sounded as if it had halted at the entrance to Hopper's ground.

This is my chance, Karim thought.

He could move around under cover of the noise. He might even try to wriggle out of the car and take a look outside.

He darted through to the front and eased himself out into the crack by the driver's seat. The bright sunlight, after the gloom of the buried car's interior, made him blink and screw up his eyes. He put his head back and felt the warmth on his face, sniffing the fresh air, like an animal emerging from its night burrow.

The vehicle's engine was still running. Carefully, Karim pushed himself through the gap, found footholds up the rubble and a moment later was standing upright, his limbs uncramped at last, able to see right across Hopper's ground.

The first thing to meet his eyes was a blue and white Israeli flag, fluttering above the tank, claiming Hopper's ground. The sight of it turned his stomach.

Then he saw the soldiers, three of them, standing nearby. He ducked down at once, aware that he was horribly exposed. He'd need to find cover if he was to watch in safety.

A little way away, an old white plastic chair lay on top of the rubble. One of its legs had been snapped right off and there was a hole in its seat. If he could only pull it towards him, and keep it steady in front of his face, it would make a perfect shield. He could look right through the hole without being seen.

He leaned forward, stretching out his arm as far as it would go. His fingers nudged the chair's nearest leg, but he only succeeded in pushing it further away.

He cursed under his breath. He'd have to take a risk, and raise himself even higher. He'd be totally visible then. Even if he could keep himself out of range, the sight of a chair, moving as if of its own accord across the surface of the rubble, would be sure to attract their attention.

He ducked down again, disheartened. He'd get back into the car and just go on waiting. The risk was too great to take.

But the idea of the chair, and of making a vantage point from which he could watch unseen, was too good to let go. And the thought of spending all day in the car, the whole day with nothing to do, was too horrible to contemplate. He had to get the chair. It was a risk he had to take.

He bobbed up a bit higher and stretched his arm out again,

extending it till it felt as if it would snap under the strain. He would be perfectly visible now to the men below. They only needed to turn around, only look this way, and he'd be caught.

His hand closed around the leg of the chair. Slowly, cautiously, he dragged it towards him. It grated on a broken cinder block. The sound shocked Karim and he stopped pulling, but the men didn't turn round. He tugged at the leg again. The chair was nearly there, nearly in the right place, just in front of his face.

Then, as he maneuvered it into the perfect position, the back of the chair caught a loose brick and sent it rattling down into the crack. It bounced noisily against a piece of jutting concrete and smashed down painfully on Karim's foot.

The soldiers had heard it. They jerked around, alert and fearful at once. Their rifles, which they'd been holding loosely, pointing down to the ground, suddenly came up. They were aiming now into the rubble, at the place from which the noise had come, directly at the flimsy plastic chair in front of Karim's face.

Karim could see them through the hole in the seat. He was holding his breath. Sweat was breaking out on his forehead. He didn't dare duck down, in case the chair shifted, or he disturbed another brick, and gave his position away. They'd come and investigate, as sure as anything, and find him, and then...

One of the soldiers suddenly laughed and lowered his gun. He was pursing his lips and making soft, enticing noises.

The others, surprised, looked around at him. He didn't say anything, but pointed across to just beyond where Karim was hiding.

Aziza was picking her way delicately across the rubble towards the soldiers. She dislodged a stone, which rolled noisily away. Leaping down the last slope, she let out a plaintive meow, then trotted fearlessly towards the soldiers.

The one who had seen her first crouched down and tickled her under the chin. Aziza rubbed the side of her face affectionately against his leg.

"Traitor! Don't go near them," Karim muttered under his breath.

All the soldiers had relaxed. The one who had first seen Aziza walked over to the tank and called out to the person inside, who appeared at the turret and handed something to him. He strolled back to the little cat and squatted down beside her, holding out his hand.

Food. She's even taking food from them, Karim thought with disgust.

Aziza sniffed at the offering, then accepted it, gulping down the tidbit and looking up hopefully for more.

The soldier laughed. Gently, he stroked her neck. She rolled on her back, offering him her tummy. He played with her, talking softly, as if he knew her already, as if he understood what she liked.

Then he looked up, his face under its steel helmet alive with laughter, his teeth showing white against his tanned skin. Karim drew in a sharp breath. For a moment, for a split second, the hated soldier, in his invader's uniform, had looked exactly like Jamal.

One of the others hit him affectionately on the shoulder, nearly knocking him over. Aziza meowed again, wanting more attention. The soldier began to caress her again, then a shout from the road brought him to his feet, his rifle once more at the ready.

Someone, just out of Karim's line of sight, called out what seemed to be an order. The soldiers swarmed up into the tank and a moment later the engine roared into life.

They'll be gone in a minute, thank God, thought Karim.

The tank began to move, its great tracks gouging huge ruts in the surface of the soccer field, but after a moment Karim heard a shouted order. The tank stopped and the engine cut out.

Karim's heart sank again. They were staying after all. They'd probably be here all day.

Noiselessly, he sank back down into the crack and edged his way back into the car. He flopped down on the back seat.

The whole day stretched before him. He could do nothing at all but wait.

The long, long morning crawled by. Sometimes, Karim tried to go back to sleep. He never managed it. He invented little games and told himself stories, trying to lose himself in daydreams. At one point, he remembered the list he'd made, of all the things he'd wanted to do and be. Was it only a few weeks ago that he'd written all that? It seemed like a year, at least. He tried to remember everything he'd written down.

All that stuff, he thought, that I used to dream about—saving Palestine, being a soccer star, creating computer games, inventing things—what a load of nonsense.

He remembered that the list of things he'd wanted hadn't been quite finished. One more item had been needed to round it up to ten. He knew now what it was. It was the only thing he wanted, after all.

Just to be ordinary, he murmured. To live an ordinary life in an ordinary country. In free Palestine. But it'll never work for us. They'll never give us back what's ours.

And he twisted and turned restlessly, trying not to make a noise.

By mid-afternoon, the sun, beating down on the roof, had long since dispelled the chill of the night and it was hot and stuffy in the car. Karim, horribly cramped and confined, managed once or twice to creep out to his viewing place again, but he only dared to move when the sounds of engines and voices speaking Hebrew drowned out the noise he inevitably made. He couldn't count on Aziza to cover for him again.

The heat had made him thirsty, and now and then he allowed himself to take a swig from the second soda bottle, but he didn't drink too much. There was no knowing how long the soda would have to last. He was surprised to realize that he'd have actually preferred water, if he'd been able to choose. The sweetness of the orange drink seemed only to increase his thirst and coat his tongue.

Aziza came and went. When she was away, he played with the kittens, tickling and teasing them, content sometimes simply to watch as they explored the inside of the car, peering after them when they disappeared under the front seats, then helping them as they tried to haul themselves up by digging their sharp little claws into the torn black nylon upholstery.

These were the best times.

As the afternoon wore on, he let himself hope that the curfew might be lifted for an hour or two, that the tanks would pull out of town to let people shop for food. Bit by bit the hope grew and grew, until it became a certainty.

Not long now, he kept thinking, looking at his watch again and again, marking each minute as it passed. They'll go at four o'clock. OK then, four fifteen. Well, that was too early. Five o'clock. They're sure to be gone by five.

But five came and went. Half past five, six o'clock, half past six. At last, Karim had to accept that the curfew would not be lifted after all. He'd have to face another night in the car.

It was at this point, the lowest in the day, the worst, probably, in his whole life up to now, that he heard his father's voice, speaking in his inner ear as clearly as if Baba himself was in the car beside him.

"Endurance. That's what takes courage. When they humiliate us, the shame is on themselves."

His chest stopped heaving. The tears dried up.

Enduring, that's what I'm doing, he told himself. In the end, endurance is what counts. And the shame is on themselves.

It was getting dark. The night stretched ahead. Restlessly, he stretched his arms out and yawned. It was too soon to try to go to sleep.

Outside, there was a racket of some kind going on, vehicles coming and going, raised Hebrew voices, the sound of a siren on a distant road.

Aziza came suddenly, leaping in through the opening. With a murmur of welcome, Karim stretched out his hand to her, forgiving her treachery at once. She sniffed at it briefly, then went to her kittens.

They'd been resting on the driver's seat, their favorite place, after a particularly vigorous game of chase. She let them drink her milk for a while, then began to push at them with her nose.

"Aziza, what are you doing?" Karim whispered. "Stop that."

The cat went on, nudging the kittens, pushing them off the seat. Ginger fell first, squeaking in protest, and Hurriyah followed him, landing in a heap on the floor of the car.

Aziza picked Hurriyah up by the scruff of the neck and half dragging, half carrying her, climbed back out through the opening, moving clumsily up the wall of rubble, encumbered by her heavy load.

Karim watched, aghast. Aziza was leaving. She was deserting him. She was going and taking her kittens with her.

"No!" he said, too loudly. "Aziza, please. Come back!"

Ginger was trying to follow his mother. Mewing pathetically, he had crawled out of the car and was attempting to scramble up the mountain of trash after her, but his legs were too short and his movements too uncontrolled. He couldn't jump easily from one stone up to the next, as she could. He stood on the lowest projecting brick, shivering with fright, making his cries for help as piteous as he could.

Karim wanted to snatch him back and hold him, keep him a hostage to ensure Aziza's change of heart. He was lunging forward, stretching his hand out to do just that, when a thought struck him.

If he imprisoned Ginger and forced Aziza to stay where she didn't want to be, he'd be as bad as the enemy. He hadn't called the second kitten Hurriyah for nothing. She had to be free to go.

Aziza had struggled up to the top of the rubble with her burden now and disappeared. Karim leaned out of the car and picked Ginger up off the brick he was clinging to.

"It's OK. I'll give you back to her when she comes," he murmured.

He wanted to hold the kitten for the last time, to feel the warmth and comfort of another living presence. He would only have the memory of it, he knew, to sustain him through the coming night.

Aziza came back all too soon. He let her come up to him and felt her head push against his hands, urging him to put her kitten down. Instead, he wriggled out of the car himself and set Ginger down at the top of the wall of rubble, taking care to keep his head hidden behind the plastic chair. Through the hole, he watched as they set off.

Aziza didn't try to carry Ginger, as she had carried Hurriyah. Instead, she went on alone, stopping and looking back, calling all the time to Ginger to follow her. He managed better than Karim had expected, slipping down between broken bricks and old tubes, struggling up tilted concrete blocks, protesting continuously with raucous little cries.

Karim watched them until they had disappeared into the darkness. Then, a little time later, he heard exclamations and laughter, and the same enticing, clucking sounds the soldier had made that morning when he'd first seen Aziza. It was too dark to see the man now.

He stood there for a long time, feeling bereft and desolate. "Winner takes all," he told himself bitterly. "Winner takes all."

Chapter Twenty-Four

Unexpectedly, although he had dreaded the second night even more than the first, it passed more easily. For one thing, Karim spent more time planning ways to make himself comfortable. He managed to wrench the headrest off the back of the front passenger seat, which, though loose, was miraculously still in place. It made a passable pillow. Then he tied the spare clothes together so that they made a kind of blanket, a real covering, much less likely to get tangled up and slip off during the night.

Oddly, he was less hungry than he had been the night before. It was as if his stomach had begun to shut down. He permitted himself a good long drink, hoping that it would help him get through the night without being woken by thirst. He had finished two whole bottles now. He'd have to be more careful tomorrow. He'd be in trouble when all the soda had gone.

He could hear noise and activity when he woke up, and it was light outside. The tank's engine was on. It sounded as if there were other huge machines nearby too, somewhere out on the road.

Karim scrambled quickly into the driver's seat. The engines might not be switched on again all morning. The opportunity to get up to his viewing place was too good to miss.

He scrambled out through the gap and poked his head up, looking as usual through the hole in the chair. Soldiers he didn't recognize were climbing up into the tank, calling out to each other. The roar of the great vehicle was deafening.

It was too deafening. He realized with a shock that the sound was coming from behind him as well, not from the main road, but from the side road on the far side of the rubble. He whipped his head around and saw, to his horror, a row of tank turrets with helmeted soldiers standing up in them, clearly visible, not more than 40 yards away. They only had to turn their heads a fraction in this direction and they would see him, as plainly as anything.

He ducked down again and was back in the car, his heart thudding, faster than he would have thought possible. Had one of them seen him? What were they shouting about now? Was it about him? Would he hear feet soon, out there on the rubble, as they set up a search for him, or would they simply blast the spot where they'd seen his head with bullets or a tank shell?

The seconds ticked by, one, by one, by one. Then the roar changed as the tanks began to move. He couldn't make out which direction they were going in, though it was away from Hopper's ground.

The sound grew quieter, then fainter still, then faded almost entirely. The column had gone, though no doubt they had left one tank behind, as before, on Hopper's ground.

Karim waited, expecting to hear the voices that he'd almost come to know, and the familiar metallic sounds as the soldiers climbed in and out of their tank, but there was only silence.

Hope began to stir. Had they gone? Was the curfew over? Did he dare to look?

He was about to make the perilous ascent up to the lookout place again, when a thought held him back. If they'd spotted his head above the rubble, they might have set a trap. They might have pretended to withdraw, to lure him out, so that they could put a bullet through him the moment he appeared. He hesitated, listening as he had never listened before.

There was no sound at all, except for the distant twitter of a bird, and the last rumble of the tanks miles away.

If they know I'm here, they'll get me one way or another, he told himself. I might as well risk it.

He moved out of the car with care, managing without the least sound, and lifted his head inch by inch, his scalp crawling with fear.

Nothing happened. No one was around. He couldn't see the tank. Hopper's ground appeared to be empty.

It's all over! he thought. I'm free!

Still cautious, he scrambled up through the crack until at last he was right out in the open and the car, his prison and his refuge, was properly behind him. Hopper's ground was empty. The tank had gone. He turned and looked the other way. The road beyond was empty too.

Karim lifted his arms above his head and stretched luxuriously, feeling his muscles uncramp. But as he lowered them again, he noticed the stillness of the streets all around and the unearthly silence hanging over Ramallah. When the curfew was lifted, the streets usually filled with people at once. They burst out of their houses, desperate for freedom and fresh air, and hurried to buy food. Where were they? Where was everyone?

His heart missed a beat.

The curfew must still be on, he told himself. Am I crazy? What am I doing out here?

He crouched down and was about to crawl back to the car when a glint of sun on moving metal caught his eye. It had come from some distance away, on the far side of Hopper's ground.

There it was again.

Karim screwed up his eyes against the dazzling morning light. What was that untidy jumble of stuff on the flat roof of the building opposite? Was it just workmen's clutter, left over from repairs? Or was it—yes, he could see now. Sandbags had been placed around the corner of the rooftop and a rudimentary shelter rigged with sheets of corrugated iron to give protection from the sun.

Soldiers must be up there. They'd made themselves a lookout, right on top of an apartment building. The flash of light he'd seen must have been sunlight glancing off binoculars, or—or off the barrel of a gun.

He was suddenly so weak with fright that he couldn't move. If they'd seen him, he'd be insane to go back down into the car. He'd be caught in there like a rat in a trap. But where else could he go? Where could he hide now?

The glint of light flashed again. Terror took hold of him and instinctively he set off, scrambling across the rough hillocks of rubble, away from the guns up there on the roof, away from Hopper's ground towards the road on the far side.

The first bullet whined past his head and smashed into a concrete block a few inches to the left. He ducked down and was for a moment too paralyzed to move, but there were only a few more feet of rubble to cross, only the last little ridge before he could scramble down the far side, where he'd be out of the gun sights, in the shelter of the wall of rubble.

He almost made it. He was almost over the top and behind the cover of the wall of rubble when the second bullet, aimed wide, hit a stone at a sharp angle, veered off it and buried itself in the back of his left leg, below his knee.

The impact felt more like a sharp blow than a bullet wound. It knocked Karim off balance, but he managed, as he fell, to lunge forward over the edge of rubble, launching himself down the other side, rolling down the rough surface, bringing stones and broken tiles with him in a deafening clatter, unconscious of the scrapes and bruises he was receiving in his fall.

He reached the bottom and sat up, dazed. As he'd thought, the rubble hid him from the gun position. For the moment he was safe. He looked down at his leg. Blood had already soaked through his pale cotton trousers and was trickling down his calf and over his shoes, staining the dry ground a rusty red. He'd hardly noticed the pain of the wound before but he couldn't ignore it now. Its sharp throb was taking him over, robbing him of all ability to think.

He rolled up his trouser leg to look at the wound. There was an ugly hole from which the blood was welling. The bullet must have gone in there. But there was no second wound, to show where it had come out.

It's still in there, he thought. I've got a bullet stuck in my leg.

The very idea of it made the pain worse, and for a moment he thought he was going to be sick.

For some reason, in spite of the warmth of the morning sun and the jacket he was still wearing, he had begun to feel chilled, so cold in fact that his teeth were chattering.

I've got to stop it bleeding, he managed to think, before I lose all my blood.

He was still wearing Joni's bomber jacket, which had kept the worst of the cold at bay during the night. He took it off and, shivering violently, struggled out of his sweatshirt. Using his teeth and hands, he managed to tear the sleeves off. He made one into a thick pad and put it over the bullet hole, then wound the other over it, binding it round his leg as tightly as the pain would allow.

It hurt him terribly, but he felt a little better when he'd finished. He'd done something to help himself. He could think a little more clearly now.

I can't stay here, he told himself. Those soldiers will have radioed the others. They'll send out a Jeep to come and pick me up.

He looked up and down the street. The wall of rubble behind him, the remains of a line of demolished houses, made up one side and on the other was a row of shops, their windows closed and shuttered. There was no shelter to be found there. But a little way up to his right, a side street went off to the left, down a steep hill. Apartment complexes four or five stories high, with strips of ground between them, lined this street. There had to be basements and underground garages there, places where a boy could hide.

He got to his feet, but the pain, shooting up from his leg as soon as he put any weight on it, made him feel sick and faint. He was afraid he would black out, and had to sit down again. Somewhere, not far away, a siren sounded. Karim lifted his head. What was he doing, out here in the open? He had to hide at once! He forced himself to move, and, biting his lower lip as the pain surged through him, he crawled to the corner of the street, and turned down the hill.

The first block of apartments, on his left, offered no hiding places. Its flat facade fronted the street, and a high wall with closed gates shut off the parking area. But beyond it a gap beckoned, a strip of vacant land running up the side and around the back of the next tall building.

The end of the wall was only a few feet away, but the distance seemed immense to Karim. The bullet lodged in his leg was making it throb with a pain that was building up and up, blotting out everything else. The blood had seeped through both the pad and the makeshift bandage now. He could feel it trickling down his leg again.

Even if I find somewhere around here to hide, he thought, I'll never be able to make it home.

He reached the end of the wall at last and looked sideways into the vacant lot. It had been cleared and readied for construction. The earth was bare and levelled, the side walls sheer and featureless.

No point in trying to look around the back, Karim thought desperately. It'll just be the same there.

He'd reached the end. He sank down onto the ground and buried his head in his hands. This was it. He could go on no longer. He'd stay here, and let them come and find him, let them shoot him, if they wanted to, or pick him up and drag him off to wherever they liked, to do with him whatever they wanted. He didn't have the strength to resist any longer.

"Karim!"

His head shot up. He'd imagined for one insane moment that someone had called his name.

I'm hearing things now, he thought, dropping his head again. I'm going crazy.

A moment later, someone was shaking him roughly by the shoulder. Karim looked up.

"Jamal!" he gasped. "Are you real? Is it you?"

"You stupid, stupid idiot," Jamal said furiously. "What the hell are you doing out here? Where have you been all this time?" He suddenly seemed to take in the paleness of Karim's face, and his eyes widened as they dropped to his bloody leg. "My God! What happened?"

The sound of a vehicle roaring up the main road towards their street galvanized them both. Karim struggled to get to his feet. Jamal hauled him up, saw him take a faltering step, then picked him up impatiently, threw him bodily over his shoulder and dived into the vacant lot. He ducked out of sight behind the building just as an armored Jeep, which had turned down the side road, screamed past.

Karim had stopped trying to understand what was happening. The breath had been jolted out of him as Jamal ran and his dizziness had returned. He slumped down wearily when Jamal set him against a wall and gave up all effort to think.

Jamal was peering around the edge of the building to check if the coast was clear.

"What happened to your leg?" he said, coming back to Karim.

"Bullet. It's still in there."

Karim's voice was shaking. Now that Jamal was with him he wanted to be allowed to stay still, to remain here, against this friendly wall, and let the sobs gathering in his chest come crashing out.

"They saw you? Where? Are they after you?" Jamal asked urgently.

"They're up there, on a rooftop." Karim pointed with his chin. "I've been hiding out in the rubble. Inside an old car."

"What, all this time?"

The respect in his brother's voice steadied Karim.

"Yes. I thought they'd gone this morning. I came out, but there were soldiers on a roof and they saw me and shot at me. How come you're here? What are you doing?"

"Looking for you, you big nerd. What do you think?"

Jamal was frowning down at Karim's leg.

"You're bleeding badly. I'll have to get you to the hospital. When did this happen?"

"Not long ago. No, ages. I don't know. This morning. I don't want to move. It hurts too much. I'll stay here. It's OK here. You go on. It's all right. I'll be OK."

He knew he was talking nonsense even as he spoke.

Jamal didn't bother to answer. He was looking across the vacant lot, his eyes narrowed, calculating.

"Look, Karim," he said gently, squatting down beside his brother. "Can you walk at all?"

Karim swallowed. Beads of sweat were breaking out on his forehead at the very thought of moving again.

"I don't think so," he whispered, licking his dry lips.

"If you put your arm around my shoulder and I put mine around you, could you hop on the other leg?"

"No, I—"

"Try," Jamal said. "You've got to try. We can't stay here. You know that. They'll be searching for you. You know what they do to curfew breakers. We've got to get to the hospital. Come on, Karim. Get up."

Karim tried to suppress a yelp of pain as Jamal pulled him to his feet and hooked an arm firmly around his body. The first step was the worst. It sent shock waves of agony right up through his thigh and into his left side, making him gasp. But Jamal's grip only tightened. Half carrying, half dragging him, Jamal forced him out into the open, towards the wall at the back of the lot.

They were nearly there when from the distance came the unmistakable droning thrum of a helicopter.

Jamal stopped for a moment as he looked up to scan the sky, then, ignoring Karim's cry of pain, he swept him off his feet and, carrying him on his back, staggered with him across the open ground, almost throwing him over the wall on the far side, where a lone fig tree spread a patch of deep, welcoming shade.

Karim hardly noticed it and was barely aware of Jamal crouching motionless beside him, as the roar of the helicopter came closer and closer, then slowly receded into the distance. He had fainted for a moment, as he'd hit the ground, and was floating in and out of a strange and distant world. Only the pain in his leg was real. His whole body pulsated in time to the stabbing throb.

For the next eternal hour, Karim could do nothing but endure. Moments of agony as Jamal half dragged, half carried him from one hiding place to the next merged with strange periods of calm, when he lay in some dusty corner as Jamal scouted around and prepared for the next dash across open ground to a new place of cover. He was vaguely aware of an oily smell as they passed through an underground garage, and later of a door being unlocked and a whispered conversation before Jamal carried him into the dark, cavernous, coffee-scented space of an empty supermarket and they could rest for a moment between the half-empty rows of shelves before their shadowy helper opened the door on the far side to let them out.

Once, Jamal had to bundle him quickly behind a row of dumpsters, holding his hand over Karim's mouth to muffle his involuntary cry of pain. Twice they almost ran into Israeli troops, knots of tanks and armored Jeeps which had taken up commanding positions at key points of the city, from where they could oversee the widest possible area and enforce the curfew.

A single word hammered in Karim's head.

Pain, pain, pain.

Chapter Twenty-Five

By the time they reached the hospital, turning in through the rusting iron gates and making a last dash across the small rough courtyard to the battered door beyond, Karim was barely conscious of where he was. Only Jamal's shuddering sigh of relief and the pungent smell of disinfectant and old grey-painted concrete told him that they had reached safety at last.

No one was in the dark front hall. Jamal set Karim down on a chair and knocked on the door of the emergency room ahead. A male nurse came out, frowning irritably.

"What now?" he said.

"My brother," panted Jamal. "He's been shot."

The man's eyebrows raised and his manner changed at once. He hurried over to Karim and bent down to inspect his leg.

"The bullet's still in there," Karim managed to say, though his teeth were chattering almost uncontrollably again. "Will my leg be OK? Will you have to cut it off? Will I be able to play soccer any-more?"

The nurse straightened up.

"We'll get this sorted, don't worry," he said. He turned to another nurse, who was hurrying past, her tired arms hugging her chest. "Tell them to bring a wheelchair, quickly. We've got a wounded hero here."

When Karim came to he was stretched out on a hard bed in a hospital ward. He lay for a moment with his eyes still shut, trying to work out where he was. The pain in his left leg, dull but insistent, brought the events of the day rushing back, and his eyes flew open.

Of course! They'd got him, with a bullet in his leg! And then, at the worst moment of his life, Jamal had miraculously appeared, had rescued him and brought him to the hospital!

He turned his head to the right. Beds stretched down the long ward, with the humped figure of a patient in every one. A couple of nurses were putting screens around someone at the far end and a woman in the white coat of a doctor was walking up the ward away from him.

What did they do to me? Karim thought. Have I had an operation? He could remember nothing after they'd wheeled him into the emergency room.

Gingerly, he twitched his left foot. The movement hurt, but it was bearable. He lifted his head and looked down. He could see the shape of his leg under the thin blanket. It looked enormous, muffled in swathes of bandages, but it was still there. He gave a deep sigh of relief. They hadn't had to take it off.

A sound from close by made him turn his head. Jamal was slumped in a chair beside the bed, his head thrown back and his eyes shut. He was snoring gently.

A tear welled out of the corner of Karim's eye and ran down the side of his face into his ear, tickling him.

He came and found me, he thought. He was out in the curfew on his own. He saved me. He could have been killed, easily.

Jamal's mouth was falling open. Karim rubbed the irritating tear out of his ear and grinned, assessing the distance to Jamal's gaping mouth.

If I had a pea or something, I could lob it right in there, he thought. That'd get him going.

As if Jamal had sensed a threat, he suddenly woke up. He gave a mighty yawn, poured out a glass of water from the bottle beside Karim's bed and took a couple of little sips.

"Woken up at last, huh?" he said lightly, handing the water to Karim, who had suddenly realized how thirsty he was.

Karim drained the glass and held it out for more.

"What do you mean, at last? What time is it?"

"Nearly six o'clock. You've been out for hours and hours. Hey, go easy on the water. The hospital's running out."

The fuzziness in Karim's head was clearing.

"What did they do to my leg? Did they take the bullet out? Where is it? Can I see it?"

"Now, how did I know that would be the first thing you'd say?" marveled Jamal.

He dug his hand into the pocket of his bomber jacket, pulled out a sharp-nosed cylinder of copper-coated metal and dropped it into Karim's hand.

"You were away in the operating room for ages," Jamal said. "They dug the thing out and stitched you up."

Karim held the bullet up and squinted at it.

"Wow. It's huge. No wonder it hurt so much. Is there—I mean, did they say it'd be OK? My leg, I mean."

"Na, crippled for life. You'll never walk again."

Jamal had been grinning, but when he saw the sickly white pallor creep over Karim's face and the shock that filled his eyes, he said quickly, "Only joking, little brother. It's a flesh wound, nothing more. The doctor said you'd be fine in a week or two. Soccer champion of the world—no problem. She says you're super-lucky, though. It missed the bone by a half inch. It would have smashed it to a pulp if it had hit."

Karim sighed and shut his eyes. There were things he wanted to say to Jamal, and a hundred questions he meant to ask, but right now he felt immensely tired and sleep was closing in on him again.

"When can we go home?" was all he managed to say.

Jamal snorted.

"How should I know? There's a curfew on, or didn't you notice? We're stuck here till our lords and masters let us go."

The next two days passed slowly for Karim. A strange atmosphere pervaded the hospital. No one could go in or out. The doctors and nurses who had been on duty when the curfew began were on duty still, their eyes darkened and ringed with fatigue. Water was short and was being carefully rationed.

"Don't even think of breathing in when I walk past," the nurse who'd first met Karim joked, whenever he came near to take Karim's temperature or change the dressing on his leg. "You'll pass out with my sweaty smell. None of us has had a shower for days and if I took my clothes off they'd walk away on their own."

The story of Karim's adventure and Jamal's heroic rescue had passed along the ward and both boys basked in everyone's admiration. Though food supplies were running low and meals were getting smaller, the nurses kept Karim's plate full and offered Jamal whatever there was to spare. Embarrassed, he took a little, but stood up and stared out the window whenever Karim was eating.

"Honorable wounds!" the old man in the bed opposite would cackle, every time Karim hobbled past to the toilets, which, without water, were beginning to smell disgusting. "I'd show them, if I was still young like you!"

Relatives of other patients, like Jamal, had also been trapped in the hospital by the curfew. They slept where they could, on trolleys or in emergency beds, at risk of being turfed out whenever a Red Crescent ambulance, its siren blaring, was allowed to bring a fresh emergency case through to the hospital.

Jamal borrowed a pack of cards and, as Karim's strength returned and he was able to sit up and move about, they passed hours in game after game, arguing over points and watching each other suspiciously for any sign of cheating.

Bit by bit, Karim told Jamal what it had been like in the car, how he'd managed to pass the time, how scary the tank had been and how the cats had kept him company. He said nothing about the soldier who'd looked so like his brother.

I probably imagined it, he told himself, and anyway, Jamal would think I'd gone soft.

They were nearing the end of an absorbing game, which had passed two whole hours of the afternoon, when Karim said suddenly, "I thought I was dreaming when you called to me out there. I'd sort of given up. I was going to let them just come and find me." He threw down the last card, conceding defeat to Jamal's superior hand, and looked sideways out the window. "I haven't really said thank you, not properly. You saved my life."

Jamal picked up the pack of cards and let them flip through his fingers.

"I did have to think about it." His teeth showed white in his dark face as he grinned. "I mean, look at it my way. I'd have inherited your entire collection of soccer posters, not to mention getting back my toy racing car which you stole from me when you were five years old."

"Hey, Karim! It's your mother on the line again!" the patient in the next bed called out, waving his cell phone at the brothers.

Jamal leaned across and took it from him, then passed it to Karim, and for the next few minutes Karim listened to his mother's barrage of questions, answering them as best he could. Lamia had been calling every two hours since Jamal had called her with the good news of Karim's safe arrival at the hospital. In the friendly atmosphere of the ward, cell phones that still worked were generously shared between the patients.

"She says she's heard the curfew's going to be off after tomorrow morning," Karim said, passing the phone back with a smile of thanks.

Jamal yawned and stretched.

"Thank God for that. If I don't eat a decent meal and get to sleep in a decent bed again soon, I'll go completely nuts."

Chapter Twenty-Six

In the end, it was another day before the curfew was finally lifted. The tanks rumbled away with the darkness of night, leaving the city just as the sun rose. Almost before the first rays had hit the dusty windows of the ward, Hassan Aboudi appeared at the end of Karim's bed. Karim, who had just woken up, smiled sleepily. "Baba?" he said. "*Alhamdu lilah!* Thank God! Thank God!"

Hassan Aboudi took Karim's hand and pressed it warily, as if it was something precious and fragile that might break at his touch.

Karim sat up and threw his arms around his father's neck.

"It's only my leg that's hurt, Baba. It's much better now. The doctor dressed it again last night. She was really kind. She's given me a pair of crutches. I'm really good at using them. She said I could go home as soon as the curfew's lifted. Did you bring the car to take me? Can we go now?"

The smell of home which floated towards Karim through the open door as he swung on his crutches up the last flight of stairs pierced him with a pang of incredible sweetness. Lamia had run out to the shops as soon as she was sure the tanks had gone, and by the time Hassan Aboudi and his sons arrived home, a magnificent breakfast had been spread out on the table. A rich mixture of hot bread, frying eggs, honey, fresh orange juice and thick olive oil hit Karim's nostrils. Combined with the familiar wafts of shower gel from the bathroom and the wax his mother always used on the floors, it made up a unique, wonderful aroma which he had never really noticed before.

Lamia hardly let him take a step inside. She swept him almost off his feet in a crushing embrace, her chest heaving with sobs.

"Oh, *habibi*! Oh, my darling! I thought I'd never see you again. Thank God, thank God you're home again!"

Then she led him to the sofa and sat down beside him, patting his hand and stroking his hair until he leaned away from her, though at the first moment the feel of her arms around him had made him want to cling to her and cry too. He had an odd feeling, as if he'd been away for a long, long time, as if the boy who'd come home was a different creature from the one who'd gone out to play soccer so many days ago.

Lamia made him prop his leg up on the sofa and brought his breakfast to him.

"So tell us. Tell us everything," she commanded, putting a plateful of fried eggs into his hand.

He fended the questions off as best he could, using his full mouth as an excuse, answering as little as possible. He'd tell her all about it one day, perhaps. It had been hard enough explaining everything to Jamal.

The telephone kept ringing. Lamia, reluctant to leave Karim, waved at her husband, who took the phone into the other room.

"I had no idea you were so popular," Jamal said, lounging over to the sofa and snatching a tidbit off Karim's plate. "The whole of Ramallah's been calling here every five minutes, apparently, not to mention Grandma, who's been going frantic in the village. Everyone's heard the whole story by now, plus all sorts of extra bits, probably, that would amaze us both."

"That was Joni," Hassan Aboudi said, just as Karim put the last bite of bread and honey into his mouth and pushed his plate away.

"Joni?" Karim said eagerly. "I'll speak to him."

"I told him you'd call back later," Hassan Aboudi said, not

meeting his eye.

"What? Why?"

An awkward silence had fallen. Into it broke the voice of the news announcer from the TV in the corner of the room, which no one was bothering to watch.

Israeli tanks fired shells into a crowded building in Rafah last night, killing nine people and injuring ...

Karim barely heard. He was looking around the table at the troubled faces of his family.

"What's the matter? What's going on?"

"They're going," Farah said, bouncing in her seat, pleased to be the one to break the news. "Joni's family. All of them. They're moving to America."

"Not America." Jamal scowled. "Amman. Jordan. Though that's bad enough."

Karim was staring at him, open-mouthed.

"Joni? He's moving? He's *going*?"

"Look, darling," Lamia said. "We were going to tell you later, when you'd had a chance to recover a bit." She shot a dark look at Farah. "George and Rose have been talking it over for months now. They've decided they just have to go. For the good of the family. They're lucky, really, that they've got the chance. They called to tell us last night."

"They're leaving *Palestine*?"

"Temporarily only." Hassan Aboudi heaved a sigh. "That's what George keeps telling me. His brother Elias is in Amman. There's a partnership waiting for him in the business. A good school for Joni. He hasn't taken this decision lightly. I mean, the Boutroses— they've lived in Ramallah and Deir Aldalab forever, just about."

"When are they going? When?"

Hassan Aboudi shrugged.

"As soon as possible. George is arranging for a cousin to take over the shop here. It'll all be done in a couple of weeks, probably."

The sofa, the room, his parents, the whole apartment and all its contents, seemed to heave in front of Karim's eyes. Then a thought struck him.

"They can't go. Not till the summer, anyway. Violette's got her school-leaving-certificate exams."

"She can do them from Jordan," mumbled Jamal.

He got up and went over to the window. He stood looking down, his hands in his pockets, his shoulders hunched, his back eloquently expressing romantic misery.

Karim reached for his crutch, stood up, picked up the phone and started to hop towards his bedroom.

"Oh, darling, your leg!" Lamia clucked after him. "You've got to be careful. You ought to be lying down."

He shut his bedroom door, blocking her voice out, and sat down on his bed. His finger was poised above the touch pad ready to punch in Joni's number, the one he knew best in the world.

He can't be leaving. He's going to tell me it's not true, he thought.

"Karim?" Joni himself answered the phone after only one ring. "Are you OK? You are so crazy! Why didn't you come back with us when we were all running away? Hey, you gave us a scare, man. We thought you were dead meat, for sure. What did they say about your leg? Did the doctors give you back the bullet? A massive one, eh, I bet?"

Karim was aware of a new sensitivity in himself, an awareness he'd never known before. He could detect guilt and embarrassment in Joni's voice, under the forced jokiness.

"Takes more than an Israeli bullet to see me off," he said, trying for the same lightness of tone.

There was an awkward silence.

"Did you... "

"Is it... "

They had both started at once and stopped. Joni began again first.

"Did you really hide out in the car all the time? You must have been so scared. Weren't you hungry?"

"Yeah, starving. But your bottles of soda helped. I owe you for that. Saved my life."

"And they didn't know you were there? You were right under their noses and they never found the car? Can't have looked very hard."

"It's all changed, Joni. The rubble's been pushed around. The entrance to the car is totally blocked. I had to go in from above, down a sort of crack. They've left an awful mess. There's ruts all over the place, and heaps of concrete and cinder blocks and stuff, right where we'd cleared it. It'll take us ages to make it all good again."

Joni said nothing. Karim could imagine him standing there, holding the phone to his ear, frowning downwards, absentmindedly kicking one leg out perhaps, not knowing what to say.

"Is it true?" Karim asked. "You're not really going off to Amman, are you? You're not really leaving Ramallah?"

He knew his voice was stiff with reproach, but he couldn't help it.

A gusty sigh came through the phone.

"It wasn't my idea." Joni sounded natural for the first time. "You think I haven't argued? I told them they could go if they wanted to, but I'd stay here. I told them—oh, what's the use? They're my family. I've got to go if they do. It's the last thing I want, anyway."

"Is it? Is it really?"

"Of course it is!" Joni's voice crackled with exasperation. "I don't want to leave home, or you, or Hopper's ground, or—or Palestine. Who do you think I am?"

"A total nutcase. Always have been. Always will be."

"Yeah, well, I'm not a happy nutcase. Ramallah's home. Always was, always will be."

"You'll come back sometimes, won't you? I mean, Amman's not exactly a million miles away."

"'Course we will." Joni sounded relieved, as if he sensed that the worst was over. "It's like Baba keeps saying, it's only temporary. Just till things get better around here."

That's what refugees always say, Karim nearly blurted out, but he stopped himself just in time. Instead he said, "Jamal's going to die if he can't see Violette any more."

Joni laughed.

"Violette's going to die as well, if she can't see Jamal. Since he did all that amazing rescue stuff she can't stop talking about him. She's just as bad as he is now."

Another silence fell.

"You haven't heard from Hopper, have you?" said Karim. "He was so amazing, Joni, you have no idea. He was throwing all these eggplants at the tanks, like they were grenades. Then, you wouldn't believe it, he ran right up to a tank and swung on the gun barrel."

"He didn't!"

"He did. On the tank's gun. I couldn't believe my eyes. Then he ran off into the camp. They were all shooting at him. I think they got his arm or something."

"They did. Above the elbow, he said. He's been at his sister's all the time, in the camp. He called me from there. He was so worried about you. Said he'd seen you fall and hurt your ankle. He didn't think you had gotten away. I called him yesterday and told him you were in the hospital, with the bullet wound and everything. He was seriously impressed."

Karim felt a little glow of pride.

"What about Hopper's arm? Is it bad?"

"No. The bullet didn't hit the bone or anything. He was super-lucky. It only grazed him. More a really bad scratch than anything else, he says. Hey, listen. Why don't I come over? We could go down there and find him maybe."

"I can't. Mama has a fit if I take a step. I can get around on my crutches, but not all the way to Hopper's ground."

"Oh, sorry." Joni sounded contrite. "I wasn't thinking. Look, I'll come over. See you in half an hour."

Chapter Twenty-Seven

I t was an hour before the expected knock came on the door.
Lamia had given up trying to keep Karim on the sofa. She did
no more than frown when he hobbled over to the door and
opened it, to find not Joni, but every other member of the Boutros
family standing there.

"George! Rose!" Hassan Aboudi said, appearing at Karim's shoulder and speaking a little too heartily. "And Violette too. Come on in."

"We just had to see him for ourselves," Rose said, looking
across at Karim as she went to kiss Lamia on one cheek after the
other.

Lamia detached herself quickly.

"Lovely to see you. Karim, get back to the sofa. You know
you're supposed to be resting your leg. Where's Joni?"

Rose looked round, surprised.

"He was right behind us. He'll be here in a minute."

It was like it always had been, Karim thought, like any of the
special days the two families had celebrated together. At
Christmas, the Aboudis had always gone to the Boutroses. At Eid,
the Boutroses had always come to the Aboudis. There had been
countless occasions, endless meals and outings. They had shared
every part of their lives.

But this meeting wasn't the same. Everyone seemed to be tense
and constrained. It might be the last time the families would ever
meet like this. The thought was unreal. Impossible.

Someone was tugging at his sleeve. It was Farah.

"Don't let Joni go out on the balcony," she whispered, her eyes pleading.

"Why not?"

"My sheets. They're hanging out to dry. He'll know."

She looked so anxious he was touched.

"He won't notice them. Even if he did, how would he know you'd wet your bed? Those sheets could be anyone's."

"He might guess."

He put a finger on her nose and pressed it. He was surprised at how sorry he felt for her now.

"I'll do a deal with you. I'll keep Joni off the balcony if you promise to keep your smart little mouth shut. No wisecracks, OK? Nobody's private affairs shouted from the rooftops."

She nodded, her face serious, her black curls bobbing against her cheeks.

"What exciting secrets are you hatching with your cute big brother, Farah?" cooed Violette, in the irritating baby voice she always used with little girls. "Oh, my, just look at your darling little socks. Pink frills! I'm going to get some just the same."

"They don't sell these in Amman. You can only get them in Palestine," said Farah.

She bit her lip and looked round at Karim, afraid she'd broken the deal already.

Karim wasn't listening. Joni had arrived.

"Hey, man."

He came up and punched Karim on the shoulder.

Everyone was beginning to sit down on the overstuffed sofas and chairs that crowded the best part of the living room.

Between them, Lamia had set out little dishes of nuts and chips on the big glass-topped coffee table.

"Well now, Karim," Hassan Aboudi said. "We're all listening. Tell us all about it. Right from the beginning."

"Not yet!" Lamia called out from the kitchen. "Wait till I bring in the coffee!"

"I'll be back in a minute, Baba," said Karim, heaving himself up from the sofa. He pulled Joni into his bedroom and shut the door.

"So what about your leg, then?" Joni said. "Is it all bloody and horrible still?"

"No, but there's a great big hole there, and it's bruised like you wouldn't believe."

"I'd have screamed and yelled and given myself away if they'd shot me," Joni said admiringly. "I know I would."

"Yeah. Well." Karim didn't know how to answer.

"What was it like being in the car, then?" Joni said. "All night and everything? I'd have died of fright, I know I would. And when they actually shot you. You must have been totally, totally petrified."

Karim shuddered.

"I don't even want to think about it any more. Like I said on the phone, if it hadn't been for your drinks—and Aziza. She was great, the first night, anyway. And the kittens. There was one soldier—he seemed to like cats. He got her away from me and fed her stuff. The second night she took the kittens and just disappeared. When she left, it felt like she was betraying me or something."

He stopped, embarrassed, as the words hung between them. Joni didn't seem to have noticed anything amiss.

"Well," he said, "Aziza made a big mistake."

"What do you mean?"

"I bumped into Hopper just now on the way here. That's why I came in after the others. I told him you were out of the hospital. He's been so worried about you. He knew you hadn't gotten away. He heard the tanks moving around and he was scared you'd hidden in the car, and they'd pushed all the rubble into it and squashed it flat. He nearly cried when I told him you were OK."

Karim grinned, pleased.

"I'll call him myself. Got any time left on your cell phone?"

He held his hand out for it.

"No, listen. There's something else I've got to tell you. When the curfew ended this morning, he went up to Hopper's ground to see what it was like and he found Ginger."

"Oh. So Aziza's still around, is she? I thought she might have taken off with them in their tank."

He couldn't keep the bitterness out of his voice.

"She didn't. They didn't take her. He saw her and the little kitten there too. They were fine. But Ginger isn't." Joni stopped and looked away. "He's dead, Karim. The tank ran him over. It crushed him."

"Oh! Ow!" Karim let out a cry of pain. He could almost feel again the soft, living ball of fur that he'd cradled in his hands, before he'd helped Ginger on his way to what he'd thought was freedom. Carelessly, callously, the machine of war had smashed the life out of him, without even knowing what it was doing.

Fighting back tears, Karim looked away.

"Hopper picked him up and took him home," Joni went on. "He buried him at his mother's place, near that patch of flowers by the door. You remember."

"Ginger," Karim said thickly. "I can't believe it. He was... "

He was so alive, he'd wanted to say.

He remembered the last time he'd seen the kitten, when Ginger had set out bravely, on his own, to conquer the mountain of rubble.

The door opened and Lamia looked in.

"Karim," she said, smiling fondly at him, "your grandma's on the phone. She won't believe you're really alive until she's spoken to you herself."

"I'll phone her back, Mama," said Karim, giving a noisy sniff.

"No, darling, she's waiting," Lamia said, shaking the receiver at him.

Karim endured five minutes of his grandmother's shouted

questions, holding the telephone at a distance from his ear, and was relieved when his uncle Abu Feisal took over.

"Well," the cracked old voice said. "So now you know how it is to be a prisoner, Karim? Even if it was only for a few hours. What did it feel like, eh?"

"Horrible, *sidi*. I hated it."

"But you survived. You didn't panic. They didn't find you. You were very patient. That's good."

"I had to be." He remembered the car's oily, dusty smell and shuddered. "They didn't crush me. I won't let them. They're never going to break me down."

A wheezy chuckle came down the phone.

"Not even when they put a bullet in your leg? You're a good boy, Karim. Now how's that handsome brother of yours? Bit of a hero too, I hear, breaking the curfew to find you. Still throwing stones at tanks, I suppose? Breaking girls' hearts?"

"I wouldn't know, *sidi*."

"That's right. Don't say a word. Brothers—you should stick together. But you tell him from me to be careful or he'll end up with more than a bullet in his leg. Is your father there? I want to speak to him."

Karim passed the phone to his father and, responding to a nod from his mother, sat down reluctantly on the sofa.

"Joni was telling us, Karim," Rose said, "about this wonderful community work you two have undertaken with boys from the refugee camp."

Karim's eyes shot up into his hairline and he turned for clarification to Joni, who had followed him out of the bedroom.

"Yeah," nodded Joni, trying to sound casual. "That's right. I was telling them, Karim, about how we'd been trying to make a sports facility so that we—I mean, you know, the kids from the camp and everywhere—could have somewhere to go and play soccer."

Lamia was beaming at Karim.

"So that's where you've been slipping off to all this while! Why didn't you tell us, darling? We'd been imagining all kinds of awful things—tangling with the Israelis, getting in with rough company, putting yourselves in danger.... "

Karim tried not to look at Joni.

"Why didn't we tell you? I dunno." He shrugged uncomfortably. "We wanted it all to be a surprise, or something. But it's all wrecked now. The tanks came in and churned up the ground and pushed loads of rubble back down onto the space we'd cleared."

"No! No!"

Joni almost shouted the words, with a force unusual for him. Everyone turned to look at him and Karim saw with surprise that there were tears in his eyes.

Karim looked away, embarrassed for his friend, and became aware that beside him Farah had stiffened with excitement. He looked down at her. She was staring at the sofa opposite, where Jamal and Violette were sitting. Jamal's hand had been edging towards Violette's and his fingers were surreptitiously closing around it.

Farah opened her mouth, about to draw this to everyone's attention. Karim dug her sharply in the ribs and pointed to Joni, who had stood up and was walking into the kitchen. Through the open door, the drying sheets could be seen on the balcony beyond.

Farah gasped, looked up at Karim and put her hand over her mouth. Karim hesitated, not knowing what to do.

In the corner of the room, the newscaster had reappeared on the TV screen.

Several prisoners were released this morning from al-Muskobiya in Jerusalem. Crowds have been gathering at the Manarah in Ramallah to celebrate their homecoming.

"Joni!" Karim called out. "Did you hear that? Come and see.

They've released some prisoners. What about Salim? Will he be with them? Did Hopper say?"

Joni came back to the sofa and sat down, his eyes on the TV. Farah flashed Karim a smile of pure gratitude.

"No," said Joni. "He didn't say anything."

Karim felt a surge of joyous energy. The news of the prisoners' release had set his heart on fire. He reached for his crutches.

"I want to go there now, to the Manarah, and see what's happening. Please, Baba, will you take me in the car?"

"Go downtown? With that leg? In all the crowds? What are you thinking of, darling?" Lamia said with a little laugh.

But the idea of going out, of being in a crowd, of celebrating something all together after the long lonely days of curfew had taken possession of everyone's mind.

"If I dropped you off quite close, if you use your crutches and take care—" Hassan Aboudi began doubtfully.

"Don't think I'm going to carry you," interrupted Jamal, with a sideways glance at Violette. "Never again. My back still hasn't recovered from the last time."

The mood of the moment had infected even Lamia.

"Wait while I do my hair," she said, disappearing into her bedroom. "I refuse to be seen downtown looking like this. Everyone's going to be there."

Chapter Twenty-Eight

Hard bright sunlight bouncing off the white stones of Ramallah's buildings made Karim blink as he struggled out of the car, which had hooted and squeezed its way through the crowded streets right into the centre of town, with the Boutros car following close behind.

They parked in a narrow side street and joined the crowds making their way to the small central square of Ramallah, where the Manarah, a pillared monument rising above four crouching stone lions, stood in the middle of a roundabout. Traffic usually choked the place, but today the mass of people allowed few cars and buses through.

As he swung around the corner with a deft turn of his crutches and saw the monument in front of him, Karim heard the drums. A procession of Scouts in sand-colored uniforms with green scarves around their necks was pushing its way through the crowd, their drummers banging out a sonorous rhythm on their huge bass drums. The sound, echoing through the narrow street, resonated right inside Karim's chest. It made him feel solemn and sad, proud and defiant.

Joni was beside him, and their fathers were following close behind.

"Look at our two boys," Hassan Aboudi was saying.

"Inseparable. I always thought they'd grow up together, like we did."

George Boutros cleared his throat.

"I know, Hassan. I know. I'm sorry. But what can I do? The future here...well... "

His voice trailed away.

Joni's fists were clenched.

"I—don't—want—to—go—to—Amman."

He spat each word out separately.

Karim said nothing. There was a distance already between him and Joni. However Joni felt about it, whatever he said, the fact remained that his family was running away.

We're not, Karim thought, with fierce pride. We're staying right here, whatever they do to us.

Borne along by the flow of people, they came out into the open square.

"Karim! Joni!"

Hopper's voice rang out shrilly over the din of the drums and the crowd.

Karim and Joni looked around. Joni burst out laughing.

"There he is! Look!"

Hopper, whose sleeve bulged where a bandage was still wrapped around his injured arm, had shinned up a lamppost so that he could look out across the crowd. He slid down again as he saw them wave, and a moment later was beside them.

"Hey, Karim," he said awkwardly. "You've gone and become a hero. War-wounded. Cool crutches. When are you going to be able to walk properly again?"

Karim grinned at him.

"I dunno. Soon. Listen, I saw you, with the eggplants, swinging on the gun barrel and everything. Awesome, Hopper. They were shooting at you like crazy. I saw the bullet hit you too."

Hopper rolled up the sleeve of his green sweatshirt to show off the bandage wound around his arm.

"Lousy shots, those soldiers," he said with grand carelessness.

"Couldn't hit an elephant if they tried." He dropped his lordly air. "Did you really see me, Karim? And were you really out there, in the car, all the time? That's what Joni said. I couldn't believe it. Actually, I saw you fall, and I thought they'd gotten you, for sure."

Karim smirked.

"Too clever for them, I guess. They didn't get me till two days later."

They grinned at each other in shared bravado, while Joni shuffled his feet uncomfortably.

"What about Salim?" he said at last. "Have they let him out?"

Hopper's face clouded over.

"Yes. He's out."

"What's the matter? I thought you'd be skipping all over the place," said Karim.

Hopper looked away.

"They did stuff to him in there. They beat him up, and kept a dirty sack over his head so he couldn't see, and he had to breathe in filth all the time. And they made him sit on a tiny little stool with his hands tied behind his back to his ankles. They just left him there. His muscles are all cramped up still. It hurts all the time."

Karim shuddered. They'd have done the same to him, worse even, maybe, if he'd been caught alive.

"Is he here?" he asked Hopper timidly. He wanted to meet Salim—tell him—thank him, perhaps, though for what, he didn't know.

"No. He couldn't face all this. Grandfather was here with us. He took him home. I stayed in case you came."

"Did you see what they did to our soccer field?" Karim asked, after a pause.

Hopper nodded.

"Yes. Did Joni tell you about Ginger?"

"Yes."

213

Sorrows had accumulated in Karim's heart and they resonated with each boom of the tolling drums. The loss of Joni, the destruction of Hopper's ground, the wound in his leg, the death of Ginger, the torture of Salim, the ever-present, ever-victorious, ever-arrogant enemy, the endless, endless humiliations—all these churned together into a morass of sadness.

The others seemed to share his mood. They stood, uncharacteristically quiet and still, as the crowd swirled around them.

"And who's this, Joni?"

The voice of George Boutros, Joni's father, broke in on them. He sounded determinedly cheerful.

Karim looked up to see that their entire two families had caught up with them and were standing all around, looking at them. Even Sireen, up in Lamia's arms, her thumb in her mouth and her head tucked under her mother's chin, was staring down at Hopper.

"This is Hopper, Baba," Joni said. "I told you about him. We've been working on the soccer field together. He's Karim's friend from school."

"Ah, yes! The community project!"

George Boutros beamed down into Hopper's mystified face. "You must tell us more about it all, boys."

"Not much point now," Karim said shortly. "The place has been trashed."

Hopper looked shocked.

"But we're going to clear it again, aren't we?"

Karim thought of the mess that had been made of Hopper's ground, of the rutted earth, the displaced rubble everywhere, the feeling that the place had been contaminated. But as Hopper's eyes held his, he remembered the moment just before the occupier's tanks had rolled back into Ramallah, when the other boys had come, and they'd all played soccer together, and he'd scored a magnificent, perfect goal, and everything had seemed worth it, anything had seemed possible.

"Yes," he said. "I guess we will."

"I'll help you," Jamal said unexpectedly. "Wouldn't mind a game of soccer myself, as a matter of fact."

Karim grinned at him, gratified, then looked away, feeling sickly, as he saw Violette give Jamal a sad, adoring smile.

"This place," George Boutros said, frowning. "Who owns it?"

"The government," said Hopper. "They were going to build something on it, my grandfather said, but they can't afford it now."

"The government? Build something?" snorted Hassan Aboudi. "That'll be the day."

"I'll have a word with someone in the ministry," George Boutros said importantly. "A youth facility—good idea. Sports— fund-raising perhaps—once we're in Amman—good contacts there—set it up properly."

He was thinking out loud, talking in businessman's code.

"I'll come along and take a look myself one of these days," Hassan Aboudi said, anxious not to be outdone. "Half a day with a bulldozer and you'd clear the place properly. Get a decent play- ing surface."

"Thanks," said Karim, looking at Hopper. "But we'll manage ourselves."

He hated the idea of the parents coming in and taking over. And he never wanted to see a big machine on Hopper's ground again.

"The others will help. Mahmoud, and Ali, and everyone," Hopper said quietly, so that only Karim could hear. The Scouts had stopped their drumming and the loudspeakers beside the platform, which had been set up along one side of the square, burst into life. The music pouring out of them, in contrast to the sonority of the drums, was fast and cheerful.

Karim's leg had started aching badly, but he felt the sound pick up his spirits and lift them, wrenching him out of his sadness. Hopper seemed to feel it too. He darted away and disappeared into the crowd.

215

"What's up with him?" said Joni. "Where has he gone now?"

"Oh, you know Hopper," said Karim. "Got some crazy idea in his head, I bet."

"You're right! Look there!" said Joni, pointing.

Hopper had wormed his way through the crowd to the monument and was climbing the scaffolding erected above it, swarming up it with practiced ease, in spite of his wounded arm.

He reached the top and waved down at his friends, and the breeze caught at the tail of his old green shirt and it flapped out away from his body, like a flag.

Karim longed to follow him, to break free from his family and climb, but he was pinned to the spot not only by his crutches but by the strange mood rising and falling inside him, tipping up and bobbing down on a mental see-saw. Up it went at the thought of Salim, free from an unjust imprisonment, but down it came again, with the knowledge of all he had suffered. It dropped even further when he thought of Joni, leaving for a new life, outside Palestine.

But Hopper's my friend, he told himself. I've got him now.

Then there was Hopper's ground, spoiled by the enemy. That was enough to lower anyone's heart. But he wouldn't let it. Not for long. He'd go back soon, when his leg was better, and he'd start again, he and Hopper, and they'd bring in the other boys, and make the place theirs again, and play soccer, and play, and play.

We'll get through all right, he told himself, waving at the boy on the crest of the scaffold. We'll survive.